Hitched

Lauren Biel

Library of Congress Cataloging-in-Publication Data

Hitched/Lauren Biel 1st ed.

Cover Design: Pretty in Ink Creations

Content Editing: Sugar Free Editing

Interior Design: Sugar Free Editing

For more information on this book and the author, visit: www.LaurenBiel.com

Please visit LaurenBiel.com for a full list of content warnings.

This book is dedicated to all my readers who will never look at a hitchhiker the same way again

This book is dedicated to all my readers who will never look at a hitchhiker the same way again

Chapter One

Lex

A shiver rakes my skin as the rain pelts me. My shirt sticks to me, the water pressing the fabric tight against my body. It's horrible, but it's better than where I came from. I'd walk through a hurricane as long as I was heading away from the guarded world I ran from.

Despite the rain worsening by the minute, I keep walking. Every bad decision I've ever made put me right here, on the side of the road, in the middle of the night. During a fucking storm.

Another pair of headlights washes over me and breezes by. I scoff, exhaling drops of water that cling to my lips. I can't be mad, though; I wouldn't pick up someone like me, either—a large, rugged, tattooed man, as dangerous as they come. A very real threat to society, as I've been told in front of a jury of my peers on more than one occasion. There are two types of people in this world: those who stop for a stranger on the side of the road and those who keep on driving.

If they're wise, they keep on fucking driving.

Regardless, being on the side of the road in this storm is better than prison. I'd endure a tsunami if it meant I was outside my fucking cell.

I had *just* gotten back my privileges when I escaped. I might have gone a little overboard with the newfound freedom they gave me. Took a whole fucking yard instead of an inch, but that's how I've always been. Men like me don't deserve freedom, but we sure as shit chase after it.

Another car drives by, kicking up mud and a torrential roar of water as it passes. I squeeze my eyes closed and try to center myself like they taught us in therapy. The *only* useful thing I learned in prison was how to deal with the things I can't control. But I hate losing control . . . now. Didn't mind it so much as it fueled the rampage that landed me in prison in the first place. Didn't mind it when the loss of control made me kill one inmate who was trying to fuck another. I didn't really care about the man pinned against the wall. But he had stabbed me, and it was an opportunity to catch the fucker with his pants down—literally and figuratively. He was too interested in the meal in front of him to notice me or the white t-shirt I used to strangle him. His last breath meant nothing to me because I was already a lifer.

The best part about life in prison was that it kind of became a free-for-all. They kept slapping more time onto my sentences, but I still only had one lifetime to give them. All that blood I shed in prison was essentially free. Anything I did cost me nothing. Even my little escape won't matter.

I'll enjoy it while it lasts, before they shove me back into isolation with only my fucked-up mind for company.

And fucked-up it is.

Selena

MY FINGERS THRUM against the wheel. I lean forward, trying to see for the millisecond after the wipers whoosh by before the rain obscures my windshield again. I hate driving in the rain, especially when it's a downpour like this. My wipers can't keep up, and the glare from signs and lights fucks with my eyes. It's already hard for me to see at night without the lines in the road melding with the rain-covered asphalt.

I pull over, flashing my emergency lights. I'll get myself killed at the rate I'm going, blindly driving down a highway at night. I turn off the car and sit in the near silence. Only the patter of hard rain against the car breaks the quiet. It makes different sounds as it collides with windows or the car's metal frame—almost like music.

Fog climbs from the hood, clawing at the windshield. There's a knock on the glass, and I snap my attention to the passenger-side window. That sound definitely isn't the rain. It's too loud and purposeful. My heart skips several beats and climbs into my throat.

The wind shifts and the rain changes direction, and that's when I see the shadow outside my car. The giant hand knocks on my window again. I turn off the ignition and lower the window a mere inch. Even with such a small gap, the rain finds its way down the window and onto the seat.

"Can I help you?" I call over the pounding downpour.

"Would you be willing to give me a ride to the next exit?" the shadow asks.

I look around. The road is empty, with deep pools of rainwater everywhere my eyes land. It's miserable outside. Torn between being smart or kind, I don't answer him. I'd want someone to help me if I was stuck in the rain. Thunder crashes and makes me jump.

"Miss, it's okay if you don't want to," he says with a smile. All I can see against the dark night are his white teeth and a soaked, light-colored shirt. "Sorry to waste your time. Drive safe." He pats the roof of the car and walks away.

I take a deep breath and watch him meander through the storm-cut beam of my headlights. Their weak glow gives me a little more information about him: he's a big guy. Massive, really, with flimsy, wet material hugging his muscles. I lean forward and watch him as the wipers make another pass.

Don't, I remind myself.

He doesn't even have a jacket, I argue back. *Nothing but that short-sleeved shirt, which is plastered to his body, and there haven't been any other cars on the road for a while now.*

No, Selena, don't even think about it.

He tugs at my heartstrings. *If he's so bad, he wouldn't have walked away,* I rationalize with myself. I take off my seatbelt, lean over, and prop open the door. The wind pushes back against my hand as water assaults my skin. I struggle to keep it open.

"Hey!" I call out. When he doesn't turn around, I beep my horn.

He stops, looks back, and seems to consider my invitation for what feels like forever as the cold rain soaks my skin. He heads toward my car. I'm tempted to close the door and lock it before he gets here, but I've committed. I already opened the door and invited him inside. The pressure of the wind comes off the door as he swings it open and leans

4

down. The dome light casts a gentle glow, and I'm able to see more of him. He's maybe in his forties. Up close, his stature intimidates me more than when he was just a giant shadow leaning into the car.

He looks hesitant, maybe because I'm younger than him. If he's in his forties, I'm half his age. Maybe he doesn't like the idea of getting in the car with someone so young.

"You sure about this?" he asks.

I focus on the way his full lips hide a hint of a smirk. I swallow hard and nod. I'm not sure about anything. This isn't like me.

He sits down, saturating the passenger seat. I feel immediate regret. It's a new car, and I didn't think this through. "Sorry," he whispers when he realizes I'm staring at the now-soaked seat.

"It's fine," I say, as calmly as I can.

He smells like a storm—a wet, polluted smell that fills the small space. He flashes his blue eyes up at me as he buckles his seatbelt and waits for my move. My jaw clenches with tension over what I've done. It just feels wrong, and his good looks only make it worse. Why would someone who looks like him be walking along the highway in the middle of a storm? Where the hell did he come from?

"Are we going?" he asks, ripping me out of my panic.

I look around and struggle with the simple motions of putting the car in drive. I can't even take my foot off the brake. "I really can't see," I say. "Can we wait?"

His eyes dart as he looks behind us. "I can drive," he says, and unbuckles his seatbelt.

I shake my head. Handing control of the car to a stranger is the definition of a bad idea. I've already compromised my safety by letting him inside the car, so I'm not about to hand over the damn keys.

He blows a breath and wipes a hand through the wet hair clinging to his forehead. "God, I did *not* want to have to do this."

My heart races as soon as the words leave his lips. The hairs stand up on my neck. My peripheral vision fades to a white blur as my body panics before my brain knows what the hell is happening. He brushes a hand through his hair, exposing a tattoo of a skull with a bullet hole right beneath his hairline.

Alarm bells explode inside my head.

The man leans over and yanks something from the back of his pants. "Either you drive, or I'll drive," he says calmly. Even though I've never really seen one this close, there's no mistaking the ominous weapon in his hand, but he doesn't aim it at me until I go for the door handle. "Don't do something stupid, pretty girl." His voice is soft, almost sensual. He isn't panicking, but his calm demeanor is making me panic.

I remove my hand from the handle and put it on my lap.

"Now drive."

Chapter Two

Lex

The fear on her face makes me feel a moment of guilt about what I've done and what I'll have to do. I hoped to carjack some piece of shit and leave them on the side of the road—probably dead—but no, I ended up in the car with a sweet-faced young girl. It isn't ideal, but it is what it is. I won't let her gender affect what I plan to do. It's all in motion, and there's no turning back now.

I grip the pistol I stole from a simple B&E on the way here. I had hoped to find some money, but this would do. It'll get me money, one way or another. An armed robbery would just be another item on my lengthening list of felonies. At this rate, I'll have a scroll of them come next week, and I have no intention of actively avoiding them. It's just who I am at this point.

A felon.

Her hands tremble on the steering wheel. There's a diamond on her left ring finger. I tighten my lips. Married?

Fan-fucking-tastic. Part of me hopes I won't have to make this girl's husband a widower, but the other part of me doesn't really care if I do. Everyone is a stepping stone on my path to freedom. I don't care who it is. I don't care who this girl or her goddamn husband are, for that matter.

"Where are we going?" she asks. Her voice is so small I almost don't hear it over the rain.

"Just keep driving south."

"I can't." Her eyes widen and breaths rush from her mouth. The fear on her face doesn't come from me, which makes no fucking sense. It's different.

I look at the purple rabbit's foot hanging from the rearview mirror and chuckle too low for her to hear over the rain. It sure isn't her lucky day. "You don't have a choice. What are you so afraid of, rabbit?"

Her eyes leap to mine, and I nod toward her good-luck charm.

"You don't understand . . ." She shakes her head as if she doesn't want to explain herself to the man with a gun on his lap, which is fair.

"Then make me understand!" My raised voice makes her tremble harder, and the car swerves on the road. When she shakes her head again, I lean over and put a hand to her throat. She squeaks as my warm skin wraps around her, but I don't squeeze. "I'm asking you once more, rabbit. What are you afraid of? Besides me." She feels so small and vulnerable in my grasp.

Her dark eyes widen, and she lets out a wavering exhale. "He'll kill me," she whispers. The words pinch past her lips, as if it hurts her to say them.

My jaw ticks. Who has this girl so damn scared? Who does she fear more than the escaped felon beside her?

I remind myself why I'm there in the first place. Her

personal life doesn't matter to me. "Not my problem. You're going to drive where I tell you, then you'll be free to go."

Her throat bobs against my palm as she swallows, and she makes a point of dropping her gaze to the road in front of her.

"That's a good girl." I pull my hand away and let my fingers crawl down her neck, nearly reaching the swells of her breasts before I pull away. I can't help stealing this moment. It's been so fucking long since I touched a woman. She's lucky I have more control than I did over a decade ago. The trip would have gone much differently then. And felt a lot fucking better.

Selena

I AM SO EXPONENTIALLY FUCKED. I shouldn't have allowed him inside my damn car. He's running *from* something, but I need to run home *to* something. The clock on the dashboard flashes the time, ticking ominously toward nine.

My phone rings, and his name pops onto the screen. My fingers rush to ignore the call, but the man beside me grabs my wrist and hits the answer button instead. I look at him and shake my head. He squeezes my wrist harder.

"Selena?" The voice blares from the car speaker. I'm frozen in fear. The man beside me slaps my cheek hard enough to shake me back into the moment, and I can only hope my husband doesn't hear him.

"Hi . . . hello, sorry, bad reception from the rain," I say, my throat tightening.

"Why aren't you home?"

"I had to pull over because of the rain. I couldn't see anything in front of me."

"You know that's not true. I'm watching the tracker on your phone. You're going the wrong direction." Accusations lurk within his words, as if he thinks I'd run away from him. I'd never be able to.

The man's face tightens. He grabs my phone off the cradle on the dashboard, drops it on the floor, and smashes it beneath his boot. My mouth gapes as the gravity of it hits me.

"Tracking you?" he asks as he shakes his head, which is really fucking judgmental for a man who's holding me at gunpoint.

"It's complicated."

He stares at me before dropping his gaze. "Drive, rabbit." He gestures forward with the barrel of his gun.

Rabbit? I *hate* that he calls me that. I don't want a nickname from him. I want to yell at him and tell him to call me Selena or nothing at all, but when I open my mouth, the words stick in my throat. I catch a glimpse of his strong jaw and realize he probably wouldn't care if I told him I hate the name. I know nothing about him, but he doesn't seem like the understanding type. He seems like a psychopath who's judging me for my life choices, but I'm not the one carjacking a woman to escape whatever they're running from.

Chapter Three

Lex

This girl will not stop chewing on her fucking nails as we drive into the parking lot of a seedy motel about an hour south of where she picked me up. It's dark and the rain refuses to let up. The rhythmic sound of the rain and the constant click of her nails against her teeth are driving me mad. At this point, I want to cut her fingers off to end the incessant noise.

"For the love of god, stop!" I shout. She slowly draws her hand from her face and puts it back on the steering wheel.

Thank fuck.

I tuck the pistol into the back of my sweatpants and cover it beneath my t-shirt. Rain pelts us the moment we step out of the car. When we get beneath the cheap vinyl awning, I pull her into me, lean down, and whisper in her ear. "Don't do anything stupid, rabbit."

"Stop calling me that," she snaps in a harsh whisper.

"Go on, rabbit. Hop." I pinch her side, and she takes a

hurried step forward with an angry blush to her cheeks. I don't want to deal with her any more than she wants to deal with me. It would be easier and quieter to kill her and take her car. By the time anyone finds her body, I'll be in Mexico.

She hasn't done anything to get me to that point yet, but it would never be entirely off the table.

We walk into the lobby, and a bell rings overhead. Wallpaper struggles to keep its grip on the walls, and what's still intact is black with mold. I look at Selena. It's clear she's never been in a dump like this before. She's wearing a slightly damp blazer and slacks, for Christ's sake. She looks clean and professional. I sure as fuck do not.

A squirrely old man waddles from the back room. His eyes jump between us. "Can I help you folks?" he asks with a furrow of his gray brow.

"We need a room for the night," I say.

"Alright. We just need a photo ID and a credit—"

"We need . . . a room." I keep my voice low and smooth as I wrap my arm around her waist. Her lips tighten at my touch, and I hope he doesn't notice that she clearly isn't here by choice. I don't need another death on my hands so soon.

A look of understanding washes across the man's face, and heat flushes his cheeks almost as much as it does hers. "Oh, *that* kind of room." He swivels his head to look toward the back room. "Eighty dollars cash will do it," he says with a flirty smile. His eyes travel down her body and overflow with hunger, and I'm tempted to gouge them out and give him something to eat that isn't her.

I clear my throat. When Selena doesn't produce her wallet, I pinch her side again. She lets out a small squeak and pulls cash from her purse.

The man cocks his head. "You okay, miss?"

I squeeze her waist closer to mine.

She flashes the man a disingenuous grin. "Yes, just nervous. It's my first time here."

"Hopefully not the last," he says with a gross smile.

I dig my nails into her side. She hasn't done anything wrong, but he's being a pig. In the broad scheme of things, I'm not much better, but at least I'm subtle about taking a moment to check out her curves.

When she brushes her dark hair back and tucks a few strands behind her ear, I notice a purplish pink hue on her newly exposed neck. Her lips are tight, and her jaw is tense. She looks so uncomfortable, which I guess is a normal response for normal people when they've been taken against their will.

The rain continues pelting the blacktop as we exit the lobby. There's an ominous silence beneath its gentle patter. A heavy quiet beneath the rain. She braces herself against the weather and hurries along, her eyes darting from one numbered door to the next, until she stops at our room for the night. 306. The six is missing, but it clearly existed at some point. I can tell by the grimy outline that remains. I unlock the door and let her inside.

Her fingers move to cover her nose, and I can't blame her. A fragrant bouquet of stale piss greets us, and the sheets look like they've been run through the same washing machine for the last ten years. The threadbare comforter has likely been there since 1963, but the television on the warped dresser looks like a newer model. The stains on the carpet bridge the gap between decades, having accumulated over the many years since this shithole was built. A roach scuttles along the baseboard. It pauses and seems to assess

Selena with the same horror displayed in her rich brown eyes.

By the look on her face and the curl of her lip, she's never been in a motel room like this. I flop down on the scratchy comforter covered in horrifying floral patterns. No matter what kind of bed it is, it has to be better than the one in my cell. The mattress releases a loud squeal as I scoot back and lean against the headboard.

"What's wrong, rabbit? Not up to your standards?" I ask, but I already know. This girl has never spent a night in less than a three star, I'm certain of that. If she's really roughing it, she might have found herself in a two, but definitely not this. I'm not even sure you can give a single star to a place like this.

She sighs, slips off her jacket, and hangs it on a hook. The metal rips from the wall and drops her expensive blazer onto the filthy floor. She picks up her beloved haute couture piece with her trembling hand and holds it away from herself as if she'll catch a disease from simply looking at it. "Disgusting," she whispers.

"Fancy little show bunny," I say with a laugh.

Her eyes shoot to me and narrow. "Fuck you." As she spits out the words, her brows furrow in surprise at her outburst. It's clearly been pent up in her throat for a while now. Her frustration makes me hard in an instant. God, she looks cute when she's mad.

I adjust the front of my pants. I don't want her to see me hard, because if she gets scared . . . like that . . . I won't be able to stop myself from doing something I will *not* regret. I'm trying to behave around her, but behaving has never been my strong suit, as my record has shown. I'm not even sure why I'm trying to be good. Why does it matter?

I had fucked-up parents—a doped-up whore for a

mother and an absentee sperm donor for a father. I may not have known him, but if he fucked my mother, he was probably fucked-up, too. I was in and out of the system since I could walk. I've never known anything but pain.

And I've inflicted nothing but pain.

She walks into the bathroom and squeals at something in there. I get up to see what she's fussing about and spot a used condom lying across the counter. I'll give her a pass on this one. It's pretty fucking gross, but I've also seen a man's intestines lying on a prison sink, so . . . Actually, it looks eerily similar, but instead of being filled with come, the intestines were filled with blood.

She backs into my chest, flailing the moment my body stops her motion. With a snared panic, she leaps away because going forward means confronting the menacing condom. Her eyes dart from the bathroom to me and back, as if she's trying to figure out which is more repulsive. I hook an arm around her waist to push her aside, and she jolts.

"Relax," I whisper. "Now you're hopping like an actual rabbit." I push past her and grip the thin edge of the toilet paper between my fingers. The rusty holder squeaks in protest as I pull. Once I've gotten enough to create a barrier for my fingers, I push the condom into the garbage. "All better," I say with a shake of my head as I walk away from her.

The stunned expression remains on her face. I've seen much worse shit than that in prison, and it will take more than a little condom to get me worked up.

She exits the bathroom like a surgeon who just scrubbed in, avoiding all contact with her surroundings. I rub the bridge of my nose. I'm exhausted. She has to be, too.

Even looking as weathered as she does, she still looks out of place. Like a rose growing in the middle of a landfill.

Beautiful, but surrounded by trash. She perches on the rickety chair as I grab my pistol from behind my back and move it to my hip before getting into bed and drawing the stiff covers over myself. She folds her arms defiantly across her chest.

"Come on." I lift the blanket on the other side of the queen mattress and motion to her. I fold the blanket over, hoping she doesn't notice the clear come stain smack dab in the middle of one of the flower patterns, as if whoever did it aimed right for it.

She snaps her attention to me, her spine straightening until she looks twice her height. "No way," she says with a shake of her head.

"I didn't ask you. It's not a question." I raise my voice. "How else will I know if you try to leave?"

She scoffs.

"It can be hunting season if you'd like, little rabbit." I reach for the gun on my hip, but I don't need to draw it.

She lets out a long breath, stands from the chair, and climbs into bed as if she's crawling into a casket. I fight back a chuckle. She wouldn't survive a night in prison. Not one single night. She'd stroke out at intake when they made her pretty little ass strip before searching every single hole for hidden contraband. I smirk at the idea and pretend I'd be the one searching her body.

She lies as far away from me as she can, nearly falling off the side of the bed to keep from touching me. She looks up at the cracked and stained ceiling, her arms crossed over her stomach like she's rehearsing her own funeral. A tear wells and slips from the corner of her eye. I wonder what the tears are for.

Is it the room? The situation? Or whatever waits for her at home?

Selena

THE ROOM BOTHERS me and the man beside me disgusts me, but I can't get my mind off my husband. I raise the sleeve of my blouse and rub the painful bruise on my right wrist. The stranger leans over and drapes an arm across me, and I flinch as he grazes the bruise that runs across my abdomen. I grip his wrist to push it off me, but he tugs me into him before I can. My body tenses, the hair standing up on the back of my neck. I worry for a moment that he'll try to sleep with me, but he keeps his crotch tilted away from my body.

I hate being in bed with him, but I'm not as afraid of him as I should be. The real devil waits at home. If this adventure doesn't end in a death sentence, my return home will. Bryce will fucking kill me.

At least the man beside me would make it quick, unlike my husband.

"Goodnight. Don't let the bedbugs bite," he says with a chuckle. I shiver at the thought of those creepy crawlers.

"Will you at least tell me your name?" I ask, knowing I won't fall asleep anytime soon, especially with the imaginary bugs crawling all over me now. Or real bugs. Real ones seem more plausible.

"Sure," he says. Sleep punctuates his voice. "Just not tonight. Go to sleep, Selena. We have a long drive tomorrow."

I DON'T KNOW how I fell asleep or when I snuggled up to him, but when I wake up and realize the warmth against my body is his, I jump out of my skin. Panic shakes me to my core, and I rip away from the bed. Breathless, I grab my jacket and rush for the door. I have no idea what I'll do if I make it out, but I can't miss this opportunity. It might be my only chance.

A metallic sound rings out, and I stop with my hand still firmly gripping the door handle. I look back and meet his dark and dangerous gaze. His pistol is trained on me.

I was stupid to think I could get away from him. Three elephants with a sinus infection breathe quieter than I do when I panic, and they're probably stealthier when climbing out of bed, too.

My stomach churns with fear, and I let go of the door, dropping my hands lifelessly to my sides. He climbs out of bed, never letting the barrel drop from me. He steps into me and fists my hair. I whimper against his rough grasp and reach for his wrists.

"I was trying to be fucking nice to you, rabbit."

"I'm sorry." I strain to get the words out. Am I sorry, though? I'm not sorry for trying, but I should have slowed down and forced myself to be quiet like the little rabbit he thinks I am.

His nostrils flare, smelling my fear as he tugs me into his body. His hand rides up my stomach, snakes between my breasts, and stops at my throat. I strain against his touch as he squeezes and threatens to block the air from reaching my lungs. My chest heaves against his huge hand. He groans and leans over, burying his face in the crook of my neck, inhaling my scent like a certifiable creep. "You have no idea the willpower it's taken to stop myself from touching you."

"I'm married," I choke out. He doesn't seem like the

type to care about the sanctity of marriage. Or laws. Or human life. It's worth trying, though. Anything is. Including my escape, I guess.

"Do you really think that fucking matters?" His breath heats my ear.

I swallow hard. "Please don't."

"Something tells me your husband doesn't deserve someone like you." His kind words contradict his harsh voice.

He's right, though.

Bryce doesn't deserve me, but I didn't have a choice. It was an unofficial arrangement between our families—a business transaction at best and my nightmare at worst. The bruises which paint my skin remind me how much he haunts my dreams. Not just my dreams, but my reality.

"Does he deserve you?" he asks as he kisses my neck. His affection chokes me more than his hand around my throat. I'd rather have his hand on my mouth than on my neck. I'd rather he kill me now than try to sleep with me.

"If you do what you're thinking of doing, I'm dead," I tell him. It's true. Even if I don't end up six feet under in some half-assed unmarked grave courtesy of this man, if I go home to my husband, I'll end up that way if this man uses me. My husband will know. He always knows everything.

"You said he'll kill you anyway," he says as he wraps a hand around my throat once more and pushes me against the wall. "So why not let me fuck you?"

My throat tightens from his words, not his touch.

"Tell me, rabbit. How many men have you been with?" His thumb grazes my jaw.

I shake my head, and he increases the pressure on my throat. "Just him," I whisper.

I was meant to be a virgin for my husband. It wasn't a religious thing. It was a business requirement.

"Do you want to be with one man for the rest of your life? What's left of it, at least."

I try to nod but his hand keeps me from moving. "Yes," I say.

But of course I don't. I haven't enjoyed sex since . . . ever. I just accepted that he'd be my shitty first and my unbearable last. I had no choice but to accept that it was my life now.

He growls, leans his weight into me, and puts his pistol behind his back. His hand rides up my thigh. My breath hitches and tears gloss my eyes.

I'm a faithful wife. I've always been faithful, despite it all. A tear slips down my cheek as I blink.

He blows a frustrated breath against my skin. "Mark my words, little rabbit, I *will* fuck you," he growls. "If not now, later. Maybe tomorrow. But for this little stunt, I *will* have you beneath me." His thumb strokes the front of my pants as his hand falls to his side.

I'm untouched. For one more day, at least.

Chapter Four

Lex

A bright sun pierces the clouds, and the car's interior is warm to the touch as we leave the motel. We start driving, and the road noise paves the way for me to get lost in my thoughts. I can't help but feel weak. I haven't had my hand on a woman in a decade. Ten long fucking years have passed without touching the delicate, addictive skin. Ten years ago, I'd have taken Selena at the motel and enjoyed every single horrifying moment of it, but I'm being fucking weak now.

Something about her seems so broken, and I don't want to break her further, which is stupid. Having always been a slave to my impulses, I've never cared about desecrating a woman before. It's taking everything in me, but I don't want to add her to my list of victims. But does it even matter? It's not like I can let her leave alive once she drops me off. I'll have no choice but to break her in the worst, most final way.

I turn my head to look at her, and every inch of her tenses. She hasn't spoken to me since I threatened to put her beneath me back at the motel. She needs to understand that it isn't just a threat, it's a promise. She had one rule, and it was for her to avoid doing anything stupid, like trying to leave. She broke that rule, so now I have to break her.

"You were a bad little bunny," I say. The more I think about her weak escape attempt, the more my frustration grows. Her lips tighten, and she refuses to look at me. "You know that, don't you?"

"Leave me alone," she snaps.

Mouthy little bitch. I take a deep breath and lean closer to her. I rub my hand up her thigh, enjoying the way her muscles tighten against my touch.

"If you keep touching me, I'll steer us into oncoming traffic."

"No you won't, sweet rabbit," I whisper. I call her bluff and run my hand across her lower stomach and slip it down the front of her slacks. As she grabs my wrist to stop me, she swerves over the center line. "Focus on the damn road," I snarl as I rip her hand off my wrist and put it on the steering wheel. Her maniacal driving is going to get us caught, which is probably what she wants. I can't allow that. "Those hands better not leave that wheel."

"Please don't," she begs. Genuine desperation pours through her strained words. It makes me hard as hell. And this is why I'm fucked up. I love how much she *wants* me to stop, *needs* me to stop.

"Please don't what?"

"Touch me," she whispers.

I smirk at her, sinking my fingers lower. "Touch you where?"

She blinks away a tear. "Down there."

I scoff. I want to hear her say it. I want her to tell me exactly what she doesn't want so I can do exactly that.

22

"You're a grown woman, rabbit. Use your words. Tell me what you don't want me to touch and why."

She doesn't speak. I'm not in the mood for these games.

"Why don't you want me to touch your pussy?" I give her one more chance to answer before I say fuck this and make her pull over so I can take her how she doesn't want to be taken.

She takes a deep breath. "Don't touch my *pussy*"—she whispers the word—"because I'm married."

I hold my hand against the warmth of her skin beneath her waistband, just above her soft mound. I'm rabid. I want to get my hands on her, sink them lower and fuck her cunt with my fingers. Even then, I consider her statement and her desperation to preserve the sanctity of her fucked-up little marriage.

And I wholeheartedly disregard it.

I lower my hand and palm her pussy. She gasps at my touch, and not in a good way. She really expected me to stop, which is hilarious. Nothing would keep me from getting my hand on her. She had to know that.

"I'm not going to play with you, rabbit. I'm just going to hold my hand here." I try to soothe the panicked rise and fall of her chest with my words. I hold my hand against her warm pussy, with two of my fingers slipping between the closed seam of her lips and resting there. I bask in her fear as she tries to drive and ignore my hand. She gets wetter and wetter with every bump in the road. She swells beneath my fingers, and I feel the contours of her clit as her body responds to me against her will.

"How old were you when you got married?" I ask, deciding she might be more willing to talk with her swollen clit beneath my fingers.

"Eight . . . teen."

"Young little rabbit, huh?" My breaths roll over her chest, and she shivers. I feel it in my fingertips.

"Has he been the only one to make you come?"

Her lips tighten, and she refuses to answer me. But I know. Her body responds to my words so fucking well. Her slick, warm excitement coats my fingers, and I fight the urge to swirl my fingertips around her clit and make her come against my hand.

"If you don't answer me, I'll touch you," I growl. She refuses to respond, so I curl my fingers against her. She jolts.

I warned her I would play if she didn't.

"Yes, he's the only one who's made me come," she whispers with a hint of defeat.

"Don't you want someone else to make you come? Don't you want to know how it feels to have another man inside you?"

She shakes her head. "I don't want another man."

"What does he do to you?" I keep my fingers still against her clit.

"Don't make me talk about it." Her gaze cuts to the steering wheel, and she tries to pretend she's anywhere else. But she isn't anywhere else. She's in her car, with me beside her and my hand on her perfect little cunt.

Selena

HIS FINGERS REMAIN between my legs, building heat even when they're still. His grasp is sure as his hand curves to cup me. I answered his questions. Well, I answered *enough* of his questions.

I don't want to talk about it with anyone, but especially not *him*. It's painful enough to remember the day my life changed forever. The day I learned who I was promised to. I knew what kind of person Bryce was and what his family was like. I knew I would live a regimented life under his thumb and that I would never be happy again. I expected him to watch my every move. But I hadn't anticipated the violence. He's an angry drunk, just like his father. The bruises on my body tell a story I try to hide beneath my clothes, and I'm not ready to share. I can't discuss my marriage or my husband with this stranger.

He won't even tell me his name, so no, I'm not telling him a damn thing, even as his fingers tease me.

I shake my head. "I'm not talking about it," I say, as firmly as I can with his hand palming me.

"If you don't, I'll make you come, rabbit." I know he means what he says by the harshness of his glare and the feral growl that leaves his lips as he says my nickname.

I think about it. I consider telling him something to placate him, but I can't bring myself to utter the words to describe my abuse. I haven't even come to terms with what I've been through. Before I can come up with a lie, his fingers dance against my clit, which begins to throb against my will. My stomach tightens at his touch.

"He doesn't . . . do . . . anything to me. He's just . . . controlling," I say through breaths that are becoming too sharp to control.

"You're lying to me." He leans his weight into me and rubs me faster. His thumb slides against my clit, back and forth, and I fight back each moan that rises into my throat. He doesn't deserve them.

My heart pounds against the wall of my chest. I don't want him to get me off, but I also don't want him to discuss my marriage. My hell at home. I can't tell what's worse. They're both terrible options that I don't fucking want.

I fight back the heat behind my eyes and spread my legs a little wider for him.

"You'd rather come than tell me about your marriage?" he asks with a raised eyebrow.

I drop my gaze from the road and nod, slow and unsure.

"Fair enough, rabbit," he says as I clutch the steering wheel. He rubs against my clit again before he opens me. He slips two fingers inside me, then withdraws his hand and rubs my unintended wetness over my clit. I shudder as my body responds to his touch. It feels so good, and that makes me feel so bad. So guilty.

A small moan leaves my lips, and it darkens his eyes.

"Does that feel good?" he asks, even though he knows. He can tell by the way I'm losing control of my body. My pelvis tilts against my will. I nod, but it's not enough for him. "Tell me with your words." He circles around my clit before brushing over it between every stroke of his fingers.

"It feels good," I whimper.

"I'll tell you my name if you come." He dips his fingers into me again. "Do you wanna know my name, sweet bunny?"

"Yes." I pant the word. I'm betraying my husband. I'm betraying myself. But he's going to make me come. I feel it brewing between my legs, rising into my belly. I rock my hips and grind against his palm as I leave my morals at the edge.

My body tenses, each muscle aching for release. I struggle to keep my eyes on the road with each forward scoop of my hips. He fucks me with his fingers, and I come against his hand. He growls as he feels me spasm around him, at the twitch of my clit. I shudder and try to keep hold of the wheel.

"My name's Lex," he whispers in my ear, his hot breath leaving goosebumps along my skin. He pulls his hand from my pants and puts his fingers into his mouth. Tasting me. He pushes his spit-coated fingers past my lips. My stomach tightens. I don't want to like what's happening. Everything inside me tells me not to.

But the hungry way he looks at me makes me want it to happen again.

Chapter Five

Lex

She's so mad at me. Or at herself. She liked my touch, and she hates that. But I loved making her come around my fingers. Her body reacted to me as if she hadn't experienced that touch at home. She probably hasn't. She probably hasn't had much positive touch in her life at all.

After feeling her come around my fingers, I want to get inside her even more. I want to feel her tighten around my dick. I want to fill her married pussy with my come.

I adjust the front of my pants without drawing her attention. I love knowing she's drenched, sitting in come that my fingers coaxed from her. She's so mad about it that her brows are permanently furrowed at this point. She hates the warm, sticky wetness that came from someone who isn't her husband.

It came from me.

A dark and dirty felon.

The black shadow beside her.

My eyes linger on her pants, and I smirk at the thought of how wet they probably are. We've been driving for a few hours, but we still have many more ahead of us. I should let her change, and I also don't mind the idea of getting out of these prison sweatpants.

"Stop in here," I tell her. She turns into the parking lot of a small secondhand store.

When we enter the building, an elderly woman behind a cash register looks up from a magazine and gives us a cursory glance before returning to her article. I look at Selena to make sure she doesn't try anything dumb, but she doesn't. Good girl.

I grab a pair of jeans from a long rack of clothes in the center of the store, excited by the promise of denim against my legs again. Such a simple thing I took for granted while in prison. Selena grabs a t-shirt and leggings and stands beside me.

"You'll want a little more than that," I tell her.

"Why? Where are we going? You haven't told me."

"Don't worry your pretty little head about that. Just trust me and get a few outfits."

I spot a skirt and hold it up to show Selena. The thin black material is exactly what I want to see her in. She shakes her head with a judgmental glare as she looks around. She grabs a pair of shorts and jeans and chooses a long-sleeved shirt and a cami from the next rack.

I walk over to her, put the skirt in her pile, and whisper, "For what I'm going to do to you, you'll want the skirt."

Her cheeks flame red as I leave her side to find another t-shirt for myself.

I search the rack, or I pretend to, at least. In reality, I'm watching her, waiting to see if she'll run out the door when she thinks I'm not paying attention. She looks less uptight when she walks now, like she's finally gotten a long-needed release and has more confidence because of it. I wonder if she'll feel tethered to my touch now that she's come from it.

Will it keep her from running off?

I snatch a t-shirt off the rack and head to the front of the store. She hasn't gotten up there yet, so I lean against a pillar and watch her again. She picks up a pair of panties that still have tags attached, but she puts them down with a grimace. With a sigh, she joins me at the front with her stack of clothes.

"No panties, rabbit?" I ask as we walk into the maze of a checkout line.

She scoffs. "I'm not wearing pre-purchased underwear. Can we stop somewhere else?"

"No. We need to get out of this area once you use your card. Wouldn't want your husband finding us. Maybe we can stop the next city over." I suddenly decide I don't want to push her panties aside to get inside her again. I don't want her wearing them at all. "Maybe you don't need any. You can go bare for me." My eyes move down her body, which trembles with renewed anger.

And I love it.

She tugs me away from the checkout line, cheeks flaming hot, her voice a harsh whisper. "What happened in the car is *not* happening again. We're not doing this. And we're definitely not going further. It's bad enough that I let you do what you did, and I'll have to live with that guilt, but I'm not adding to it."

"Sweet bunny," I coo, "you think you have a choice regarding what I do to you? How adorable." I brush a hand against her cheek, and she rips away from my touch. Her lips tighten and her bravado deflates in front of my eyes. "You shouldn't have let me feel you coming around my fingers, because now I want more. No, I *need* more. So when I tell you that you aren't going to wear panties or that you're going to wear that little skirt, you're going to listen. I'll make you feel better than your husband ever did."

Her eyes darken. She doesn't realize just how long it's been since I've felt the soft warmth of a woman beneath me. She doesn't understand how obsessed I am with the thought of touching her again. It's an obsession that started once I felt her, once I reveled in the warm rush as she came against my hand. She had tried to run, just like a scared little rabbit. But I would tame her.

"I'm going to shower," she says with a glance toward the bathroom. Yet another room that isn't up to my little rabbit's standards.

"Get undressed in here," I tell her with a smirk.

She clutches her clothes to her body, shaking her head in a stiff motion. I consider forcing her to strip in front of me, but her eyes well with tears. I tighten my lips. I have no idea what's wrong with that girl, but I'll find out.

"Go on, rabbit." I wave her off. I won't force her to tell me what she's been through . . . yet. Some people come out stronger when you force them to confront their pain, but others break. She seems like she'd break. She isn't strong enough to confront it on her own, and I'm not the person to make her stronger.

Selena

I breathe heavily against the cracked faux marble countertop in the bathroom. The lights flicker above my head with a low hum that grows louder with every passing moment. I've been so afraid he'll force me to undress, but not because of the infidelity. I fear seeing his expression as he becomes aware of the bruises on my body. I don't want to see the look of pity on his face.

Whenever someone catches a glimpse of my marks, they get that same look, but they don't do a goddamn thing about it. They probably think I did something to deserve it.

Bryce is a saint, and I'm the pitiful sinner.

I take a deep breath and lock the door before removing my blouse. Each unfastened button reveals more of the fresh purple bruises on my chest and stomach. When I slip the sleeves off, my eyes find the older bruise encasing my wrist. I remember the fight that caused the deep pinkish-purple mark. I remember every stupid fight. How could I forget when the proof of each one marks my skin? I touch the one on my stomach. *I wasn't home in time to make him dinner.* I graze my chest. *He forced me to fuck him because he had a bad day at work.* I grip my bruised wrist. *I took too long to get ready last week.*

I slip my slacks off, exposing a mixture of old and new bruises on my thighs. A near-perfect handprint decorates my inner thigh, almost reaching my crotch. I shudder when I remember how he fucked me to give me that mark. I flinch as I touch the yellowish bruise above my knee, where he kicked me when I was already down.

When I'm dressed, I feel like a normal wife. When I'm naked, I understand why I'm not more upset about sleeping in this scuzzy motel room instead of beneath the expensive sheets embroidered with golden threads. Those expensive sheets mean lying beside Bryce. The man out there, Lex, is on the run from something awful, and I still felt safer in bed with him last night than I ever had with my husband.

And that's fucked.

I turn on the faucet in the tub. Brown water rushes out as the pipes rattle behind the wall. It finally runs clear, albeit cold, but I get in anyway. Standing naked in the disgusting bathroom just makes me feel dirtier by the moment.

My eyes lock ahead as I clean myself, focusing on a crack that races up the wall across from me. Mold straddles it and follows its path.

A knock at the door breaks me from my trance. "I'm almost done," I call out.

When I get out of the shower, the leggings and the long-sleeved shirt I got at the store wait for me on the counter. I narrow my eyes. I'm certain I locked that door. I pick through my discarded clothes on the floor and discover that my panties have vanished.

Fucker.

"How'd you get in?" I ask as I step out of the bathroom, motioning toward the clothes I put on. He just shrugs. "And where's my underwear?" I ask.

A fierce sexual frustration shines in his eyes at the sight of me. I hate that he looks at me like that, in a way my own husband never has. I hate that I like when he bites his lower lip as he openly scans my body.

"I told you. I don't want you wearing any." His gaze leaves me and turns to the television. He knows just how to draw me into wanting his attention, wanting to be more interesting than the grainy picture on the old TV. But not so interesting that he might want to touch me.

I open my mouth to argue, but the words stick under my tongue. I close my lips, thinking better of what I want to say.

Lex's eyes leap to mine when he sees my wordless response, and the breath catches in my throat at the intensity of his stare. His expression becomes feral and animalistic, and I know I should tread lightly.

"You want your panties, rabbit?" he asks.

I nod, even though I know I shouldn't. Not when he's looking at me that way, as if a sadistic idea has just crossed his mind.

Lex gets up, reaches into a drawer, and pulls out my black underwear. He stares at me as he sits down, unzips his jeans, and tugs his cock from the spread wings of denim. A smirk crosses his face. As menacing as it is, it's wickedly attractive.

His eyes never leave my face as he strokes himself, slow and intentional. Saliva gathers under my tongue at the sight of him, but I force myself to remain stoic. Even so, he's noticed the subtle nibble of my lip, because his movements grow rougher and more determined.

"Do you like what you see?" he asks.

I want to shake my head and tell him no, but I'm frozen. I force my body to obey me enough to sit in the stiff, squeaky chair facing the bed. The TV show flashes across my peripheral vision as I watch him.

My eyes rove over the huge cords of muscles from his shoulders to his biceps, which flex with every stroke.

"Do you know what I like, rabbit? When it's not a no from you, it's a yes. Shit, even when it's a no, it's still *my* yes." He brings my panties to the head of his cock. He drops his head back and groans as he comes in my underwear, saturating the thin fabric. "We're going to have so much fun together, you and I." Lex smirks as he tosses the panties onto my lap. "Well, put them on."

I shake my head before he even finishes his sentence. Absolutely not. I will *not* put his come against my skin. "I'm not wearing those," I say, as firmly as I can muster.

"Ah, no, that's not how this works. You wanted your goddamn underwear so bad. Put them on." His smirk tightens. "I'm not asking you again." The way his jaw tenses and pulses, I know I have no choice.

He's forcing me to take what I wanted in the first place.

I swallow and stand up, taking the panties to the bathroom because I refuse to change in front of him. I can't.

I wipe off some of his come, but the wetness is too embedded in the fabric. When I slip them on, I feel his warmth against my skin. It makes me shiver. When I return to the bedroom, his eyebrow lifts as he tucks his spent cock away.

"Show me that you're wearing them," he says.

I hook the front of my leggings and lower them enough to expose the black silk. Satisfied, he relaxes and starts watching TV again.

When I sit down, the damp area is more noticeable. It's become a bit cold. As hard as I try, I can't ignore his pleasure against me. I cross my legs and cut my gaze to the stained carpet at my feet, trying to talk down the throbbing ache he's caused. Several cigarette burns surround the stain. The place is a dump, and it's easy to get lost in the mess of it. But even then, *his* mess in my panties still stays the center of my focus.

Lex's presence haunts me from across the room, and my eyes ride up to him once more, taking in every contradiction that makes him somehow attractive and disgusting at the same time. The stubble on his chin looks rough, but it still works with his otherwise sweet features. He only looks as mean as he does because he never smiles from joy. He smiles to get his way because he's a manipulator. His voice is so low and sexy, but it only masks the threats woven through his words. He isn't nice or kind. He's a bad fucking person, and he's forcing me to wear him.

Lex brushes a hand through his thick hair as he lets out a breathy laugh and stares at the TV. "I don't like when you stare at me," he says without looking away from the television.

"I don't like to wear your come," I mumble under my breath.

He puts on a smile and motions me to him. I keep myself planted in the horrible motel chair.

"Now," he commands. He has a voice he uses when I have no choice but to listen, and that word drips with his demand. I stand up and go to his side, and he rubs his hand between my legs and bites his lip. "Oh, bunny, you're going to wear those panties to sleep and then they aren't coming with us." He grazes my slit. "How does my come feel?" he growls as he fists my hair and draws me to his mouth. His lips stay far enough away from mine to accomplish little more than pissing me off. My dark hair in his grasp is still wet, and drops of cold water fall down my shoulders and make me shiver.

"It makes me feel gross."

"Get used to how I feel, because I can't wait to see you covered in my come, sweet bunny."

"We aren't doing more," I say, pushing my hands against his chest.

Lex growls—a carnal sound that makes me weak. "I love how you think I won't end up inside you. I may have to tear you apart to get there, but I will get inside. Tonight, I'll leave

37

your vulnerable little underbelly alone. But soon, nothing will keep me from ripping you wide open."

He releases his grasp on my hair and pulls his hand from between my legs. He pats the vacant side of the bed. The swirl of arousal I feel leaves me more confused than ever.

He lifts the blanket and stares at me, but I shake my head. There's another bed this time. I don't need to sleep with him. I get up and lift the blanket on the other bed before climbing into it. When I turn over, I hear rustling, then the whoosh of cold air as the blanket lifts away from me. His warmth engulfs me as he gets into bed and lies on his back behind me.

"If you don't want to come to me, I'll come to you. I don't trust you. You might try to scurry away again, little bunny."

I won't run off, even though everything in my body tells me I should, especially the wetness between my legs.

Not only his, but mine, too.

Chapter Six

Lex

I wake up in bed, all by myself. I sit up and look for Selena, certain she's taken off. Apparently, she figured out how to be a quiet little rabbit after all. I relax when I hear the running shower. *Good girl.* She can clean herself all she wants, but it won't be the last time I cover her in my come. She may have shed her panties, but I love that she slept—at least for a while—with my come against her skin. I like that she's so torn between liking it and hating me.

She needs to learn, though. I won't allow her to have her panties unless she's wearing me, too.

After her shower, we load our things into the car and set off again. Hours later, she sits beside me, staring out the passenger-side window as the sun sets. She hasn't spoken to me since we started driving.

"Are you really still mad about your panties?"

She doesn't look at me. "It's not about *what* you did. It's *why*."

Oh, she speaks.

"Tell me *why* it bothered you, then."

Her eyes roll and it reminds me how young she is. How naïve and innocent she is. "Because you want to own me. And I'm not someone's to own."

"You have no idea what it means to be claimed by me, sweet rabbit."

Her eyes flash to mine, fear radiating from them. "We *aren't* going further. Wishful thinking isn't going to get you inside me, Lex. There's absolutely zero chance of that, so let it go." She wants so badly to believe the words coming out of her mouth. She wants me to believe them, too.

"I don't need wishful thinking." I tap the rabbit's foot. "And I don't need luck, either. I *will* bury my cock inside you before this road trip ends. I promise you that."

Her cheeks flame red at my words. Despite reining in the side of me that would take her against her will, I will unleash that side before we reach my destination. Even if I didn't have to kill her, I'd make sure I released her back to her husband with my come dripping from her.

We take a turn onto another back road, and then another. That's all we've been doing, and it makes the drive feel like an eternity without enough progress to make our stiff knees and numb asses worth it. I pull into a familiar-to-me parking lot. I could use a chance to stretch my legs, and I need an ID—something I can use to cross the border without suspicion. I'm too big to hide in the damn trunk.

I'd been in prison for a decade before my escape, so I don't have the connections I used to, but I know a man who makes them. He was a fairly unsavory character, even by my standards, but Rodney has the means to provide what I need. I drag us to his doorstep, hoping he still lives in the rundown apartment complex. Unless he's in prison, he should be here.

I knock on the heavy metal door, and it opens after several locks unlatch from the other side. Rodney looks at me like he's seen a ghost, his face paling in front of me. "Lexington Rowe, do my eyes deceive me? I thought you were doing life, man!"

"Don't call me that, and fuck off about my business," I snap. I hear the gasp beside me as Selena learns more of the secrets I have yet to reveal. She has to know, on some subconscious level, that I'm running from the law. She probably doesn't expect my crimes to have earned me life, though. Well, several lifetimes.

I can't deal with her feelings right now. This isn't a place to feel and look weak. Rodney will feed off that. I'll try to explain it to her later when we aren't in front of another felon. When I can answer some of the questions I'm sure she'll have. It's the sort of conversation I would never have in front of fucking Rodney.

I push past him, and he stares at Selena as if she's a steak laid out in front of him. Maybe even better than a steak. She's something so mouthwatering that he can't take his eyes off her. Admittedly, she looks fucking delicious, with her youthful innocence and prim appearance, even when she isn't dressed all proper.

I'm certain of very few things, but no one is getting a bite out of her before I do. She's my meal, and I'll slit a man's throat if he so much as sniffs her sweet scent before I can take a huge chunk out of her to fill myself with. I grab her arm and pull her into me in a protective gesture. It's not my usual way, but I feel compelled to do it. That innocence needs protecting.

"Does she need one, too?" Rodney asks, his eyes still crawling over Selena's body. He's eyeing my little rabbit like a coyote looking down at his prey. His expression relays his thoughts clearly, and he can fuck right off as far as I'm concerned.

"Just me," I tell him. "What have you been up to, anyway?" I ask, trying to draw his hungry eyes off Selena, whose cheeks have flushed under his dogged staring. It's painful for me to witness. It's like he's never seen a woman in the flesh before.

"Living the dream," he says as he wrenches his eyes away from her to finally look at me. "Served three in county for some fraud charges, but I'm back in business. My nephew stayed here and kept shit running while I was locked up."

"How much for a new ID? Or passport. Anything I can use to get my ass out of the states."

"There's time to talk business. Come with me to take a picture first." He dodges the question precisely how I expect him to. He'll keep dodging until I get too far in the process to back out, forcing me to pay whatever he asks. I push him for a price, but he just keeps avoiding the question like the expert piece of shit he's always been. He's a bottom feeder, lower than me, and I thought I was pretty fucking low.

Rodney snaps my picture and leads us into a room where he sits in front of his fancy multi-computer system. The lenses of his old glasses reflect the screens, their joints bent out to accommodate his round, wide head.

Selena and I take a seat on the couch, but she refuses to look at me. Her arms are folded across her chest like a defiant child. Which I deserve, but not here. She can't look like a child, because that's precisely what a dude like Rodney would. When I say he's unsavory, I mean . . . fucking vile. I'd have left Selena in the car if I wasn't worried she'd be hunted in the parking lot by one of the many violent sex offenders in this complex. Honestly, if you pull up the predator map, you wouldn't even know there's a building here beneath all the red dots. Rodney's big, stupid mug would be buried somewhere in all those warnings.

I'm being real judgmental of a fellow felon, but at least I have a line I won't cross.

That reminds me of the questions I'll have to answer later. I should have let Selena hear my past from my own mouth. That would have been the mature thing to do, but I didn't want to give her more information to use against me if she somehow got away from me. She'd probably try to run once I told her, because that's how a normal person would respond. They'd run.

Despite what she thinks, I'm as happy to be in this situation as Selena is. It would be much easier if I killed her and took her car. I wouldn't have another human being to worry about while on the run. Things would be a lot less complicated if I wasn't always thinking about finding ways to get inside her.

"Earth to Lex?" Rodney snaps his fingers in front of my face before shoving an ID into my hand. "How's this?"

It looks and feels legit, and my scowl is pretty accurate.

"You failed to tell me how much," I say, putting pressure on the card between my thumb and forefinger. Rodney is a sneaky fuck, and I intended to stop him from printing shit before I got the price. I was too busy lost in thoughts of Selena to notice the sound of the printer firing up. This is what I mean. Less complicated.

"I told you, but you were staring off in la la land," he says with a dry laugh. I missed some of the shit he'd said, sure, but I would have noticed that. "It's one grand for you."

My mouth falls open. *Sneaky fuck.* "Since when has it ever been near that price?"

"Since New York switched their ID format and you became desperate enough to pay for it." A gross smile crosses his face. Oh, fuck him. Even someone like her wouldn't have that kind of money on hand. But he's right. Desperation always costs extra. That's the way the game is played.

"We don't have that, Rodney, and you know it," I say as I stand.

He meets my stance but hardly reaches my chest. He brushes a hand through his balding hair. "You have something I could take as payment." His hungry gaze drops to Selena.

Her eyes widen as mine narrow. I fucking knew those words would come out of his mouth. As soon as I saw him drooling over her, I knew he'd try to order her off the menu. He knows we have to work off the cost somehow, and he sure as shit wouldn't want to fuck *me*.

I'm torn. I don't want to give her away like that, even for a quick fuck, but I also *need* that fucking ID. There's no way around this. I'm not going back to prison. Giving her away for my freedom seems like a small sacrifice. It's one I have to make.

I cut my gaze and sit on the couch with a harsh exhale. Selena's eyes fill with betrayal. I can't look at her, but I feel the desperation as she fights against his grasp when he reaches for her. He finally gets his hands around her wrists and drags her to her feet, pinning them behind her.

"Fuck you, Lex!" she screams. Hatred radiates from her with the heat of a thousand suns.

I deserve it.

He puts his palm around her mouth, muffling her

screams, and I drop my head to my hands. Does he have to do it right here? Does he have to dangle her fear and desperation in front of me?

"Shh, honey, I'll be quick," he whispers in her ear as his free hand works down his jeans. Once he gets the denim past his ass, he works down hers. My eyes leap to the pale skin of her ass as he pushes her against the wall and pins his weight into her. I swear I see the haze of a bruise on her skin, but it might have been the light from the computer screen.

I force myself to look away from her ass, and my eyes rise to her eyes. They're swollen and red with fear, the glaze of her tears coating them. I shake my head, trying to keep my hand away from my pistol.

I have to let it happen.

It needs to happen.

There is no freedom without it.

This has never bothered me before. In fact, I like glimpsing fear on the face of a beautiful girl. I always have. But this is bugging me. Really gnawing at my nerves. The burn beneath my skin is a foreign feeling for me, and I don't like it.

My muscles twitch and I struggle to keep them still. Her muffled screams wiggle between my ears and gnaw at me like sharp little rabbit teeth. I reach back for my pistol, but I can't bring myself to grab the grip. It would be too loud and messy, and the cops keep their eyes on this shady complex. They practically live on the premises at this point. Instead, I leap up while he's too busy prodding between her legs with his tiny dick and panting like he might come before he even gets inside her.

That'd be convenient, actually.

I wrap my arm around his neck, and he releases Selena

45

the moment I grab him, his hard dick softening as I choke him. His hands claw at my wrists, and he flails against me. It's eerily similar to how she struggled against him. My lips purse as I keep a steadfast grasp on his neck, refusing to let him get half a breath.

Selena pulls up her pants, her chest heaving as she runs for the door.

"Don't you dare, rabbit. There'd be another one just like him waiting for you." My words come out strained as I struggle against the weight of a man fighting to live.

She stops, her hand on the doorknob. She has to know that darkness just veils monsters—monsters like me and definitely like him.

I get sick of the struggle. I release Rodney enough to get a grip on his head and snap his neck. The familiar crack rides up my spine, and I lower his body to the ground, wiping at the blood on my arms from him clawing at me. I look at Selena. Her eyes are full of deserved mistrust. I put something up for sale that didn't belong to me. She snatches open the door and bolts from the apartment. With a shake of my head, I grab the ID off the floor and follow her.

"Rabbit!" I call after her as she races to the car. I quicken my pace to catch up with her. When I'm close enough to grab her, I slam her against the car, turning her to face me. Forcing her to look into my eyes.

"Fuck you," she cries. Her body trembles, and fear courses through her. She's still trapped in that moment with him, even away from the apartment. Her hard glare bites at me. I deserve to be bitten like that, but her words still piss me off. I'll meet her bite with a stronger one, and she knows me enough to know that.

I lean into her, putting a hand to her delicate throat. The whites of her eyes are all I can see in the dark parking lot. She saw what I'd done in one swift motion, and here I am, with my hand around her fragile little neck. "Don't be so fucking mouthy, rabbit," I say. I feel the throb of her heartbeat beneath my fingers. Nervous sweat coats her skin.

"You tried to sell me!" she says with a strained voice.

"More like . . . loan you." I'm trying to rationalize with myself as much as her. What I did was fucked, yes, but sometimes there's no changing who you are, even in the face of something so different from what has molded you.

Her skin is hot, heated by anger and . . . something else. It courses through her veins. She inhales sharply, looking up at me with an emotion I've never seen from a person.

It's the look of someone who has just cracked.

"Kill me." Her voice comes out small and weak, but somehow still sure.

I raise my eyebrow, but I doubt she can see it in the darkness. "What?"

She lets another warm breath wash over me. "I said . . . kill me." Her voice wavers this time.

I lower my hand from her throat and rest it on her clavicle. She's taken the fun out of preying on her. Her fear has mutated into surrender in front of my eyes, an over- whelming feeling of brokenness that washes over us both. It's contagious. And I can't say that I've ever felt such sadness, even as I was beaten half to death as a child or when I knew my life was over as I stood before a judge. This feeling is foreign and uncomfortable, and I can't imagine living in that eternal state like she must. I understand why she wants to die.

If she dies, that emptiness dies with her.

"Is that really what you want, bunny?" I ask, letting my free hand move her sweaty, dark hair from her cheek.

"I'm as good as dead either way. I don't want to play this

game anymore. Take the car. Do whatever. Just . . . I can't . . . do this." Her world is collapsing around her, crushing her. And it's all my fault. Well, not totally my fault. Clearly, her husband is a fucking cunt. He broke her before I took her, but I created the final crack that split her wide open.

I lean into her, putting my forehead against hers as I drop my hand from her chest. "Get in the car, little rabbit," I whisper. "The backseat."

She hesitates before she grips the handle and crawls into the backseat. I scoot her over and sit beside her. "Are you sure that's what you want?" I ask as I lean into her and rest my hand on the curve of her neck. She has such a fragile throat. I hardly noticed that before tonight, and suddenly it's all I can think about. How she's like glass in my grasp. But if she really wants this, she picked the right person to ask. I'm the only one who can do it without thinking twice. Without losing sleep. It is and always has been too easy for me to take a life.

The dome light cuts off, blanketing us in darkness, and I feel the warmth of a tear trail over my hand. Except for some soft sniffles, it's sickeningly silent. She nods her head, and I feel the motion within my grasp. She seems so certain, leaving me to think about it. My muscles twitch, and I yearn to give her the release she wants.

I lean in and whisper, "If it's what you want, I'll do it for you." My voice wavers, which is uncharacteristic of me. I feel doubt in my gut, some nagging discomfort I've never felt with any murder I've committed. And it *is* murder, even if she wants to die.

My hands ride higher to grip both sides of her head. She relaxes into my touch, as if I'm giving her a gift. To her it is. To me, it feels like a burden I don't want to bear. But I will.

I take a deep breath.

It's what she wants. It's for her. It's all for her.

Selena

I FEEL the heat of his hands on either side of my head, but his touch doesn't burn me like it should. I don't dare take a breath as I wait for the sharp twitch of his muscles before nothingness. It isn't that I *want* to die, but I'm just so fucking done. So tired from it all. Bryce *will* kill me when I get home. He'll end me in the worst, most painful way he can muster in his sadistic mind. It seems better this way.

As crazy as it sounds, it feels safer.

With closed eyes, I bathe in the blackness behind my eyelids. I need to sleep. I need to rest. And I'll never get that from the life I have, even before Lex took me. There's only one ending for me. There has always only been one way it could end, and it's this way: death at the hands of a man. I'm just choosing whose hands it will be.

His hands fall from my face, and he leans in to kiss me. I draw away from him, catching his breath on my inhale. He tastes like sin.

"Lex," I whisper as I push at his chest.

"If you still want to die after I fuck you, I'll do it for you." His voice is low and desperate. "Let me inside you, rabbit."

How much lower can I go? Past the six feet under I hoped for? Sleeping with him will send me on a free fall to hell, but does it really matter at this point? How important is the sanctity of a marriage that leaves me covered in bruises?

I drop my shoulders as he leans in again. The moon peeks through the windshield, offering mere glimpses of weak light. He won't be able to see my marks. He can't pity me. I can pretend to be an unmarked woman for once in my life. I can pretend I'm a normal twenty-two-year-old. I might even find a few moments of happiness.

His lips meet mine again, and I accept his kiss. I spread my mouth to let him inside. His chest rises heavily as he leans over me, pushing me against the door as he crawls between my legs. His hand wraps around my neck and rises to grip my hair. He tugs my shirt off, letting a heavy hand slip over the swells of my bare breasts. I fight the flinch of pain as his touch runs over the bruises near my waistband. I'd never let him do this if he could see me. I don't want anyone to see just how damaged I am. He tugs down my pants with the hunger of an animal at the end of its leash, and it's about to break.

I hear his zipper fall.

It's becoming real.

It *is* real.

I gasp as I feel the warmth of his cock against my pussy. I want to stop him. I reach out and push against his broad chest, but he's so strong. So *much* stronger when he's above me. "Lex," I pant, the hesitation woven through the word. It feels like it's too late. The leash is hardly holding him back now, especially when he's so close to slipping inside me.

"Shh, sweet bunny," he whispers before kissing me again. "Let me in." He growls and deepens the kiss. His firm hand explores between my legs, and I lurch into him as the touch sends electricity through my body and awakens things that have long been asleep. Maybe these parts of me had never been awakened at all.

His fingers push inside me, a touch that my body remembers. I curl my hips against his hand. He draws his hand away, and I hear him spit. He touches me again, sinking his fingers inside me. I can't see his cock, but I feel its heat against my skin. I remember how it looked at the motel. Like the rest of Lex, it's huge. I wish it wasn't so damn dark so I could see him. But if I could see him, he could see me, too.

And that can't happen.

When he pushes inside me, stretching me in ways I've never felt, I scream out, partly from the shock, but also from the realization that someone besides my husband is inside me. Ripping through me. Making me everything my husband says I am.

A whore.

A slut.

"God," he groans as he pushes deeper. "Your husband is so fucking stupid." He whispers these words before drawing back to the tip and pushing into me again. My nails dig into his sides as he fucks me, slow and sweet, in ways I don't expect. It doesn't seem like he'd fuck me this way. "Don't worry, sweet bunny. If you let me keep you alive, I'll show you how I truly fuck. I'll give you a reason to take that next breath for me," he growls, as if he senses what I'm thinking.

I melt against the door, the armrest stabbing my back in the cramped space. It doesn't matter, though. I close my eyes and allow myself to focus on the friction between my legs as he thrusts in and out of me. I listen to his deep, desperate breaths as his hips drive into mine. He shows me only a fraction of his strength, and it frightens me as much as it excites me.

He pulls out and sits down, pushing my legs out of the way. "Get on my lap," he commands in a breathy voice that makes my legs weak for a moment. I feel for him in the darkness and straddle his waist, my head nearly hitting the roof of the car. He twitches against my pussy. "I want to see you," he whispers.

His hand moves toward the dome light, but I grab his wrist and place his palm on my ass instead.

"Leave it off," I say as I put him inside me. I don't want him to see the bruises now, after his hands have raced over every sore part of me.

"I'm going to get my eyes on your body, little rabbit," he growls against my mouth as I lower myself on his cock. My heat rides down to his pelvis, and the groan that leaves his lips makes me throb. My moan breaks through the static silence.

"Not now," I whisper, my lips hovering in front of his.

"What are you hiding from me?" He bucks his hips into mine, and his huge arms wrap around my body. I feel so small in his grasp. "What don't you want me to see?"

"Leave it alone, Lex," I say as I slow my movement on his lap, nearly stopping as he forces me to confront what I refuse to. Not now. Not when this moment is so perfect.

"It's going to piss me off, isn't it?" He pulls me into him until my naked, sweaty chest presses against his. My hips stall their motion, the weight of his questions bearing down on me. "Don't think about it right now," he says. "It's something for another day." He kisses me, and it's sweet. I'm surprised he's capable of that. Being sweet.

The recently formed memory of him giving me away to that man—and then killing him—rushes to the front of my mind and contradicts every bit of this sweetness.

"You were going to let him fuck me," I whisper as I drop my head into the crook of his neck.

"I know, rabbit." He lifts his hips to meet mine. "When I saw him about to take what I've wanted . . ." He releases a frustrated growl. "There was no way I could leave him breathing. No way I could let him feel you around his dick before I felt you around mine." He kisses me so hard that it makes me whimper. "But now that I've been inside you, no one else will ever be, including your fucking husband."

With his possessive words in my ears, I ride his cock and inch toward an orgasm. It's been so long since I came during sex. Before he made me come with his hand, it'd been so long since I felt that kind of pleasure at all.

"You're tightening around me," he says, and I know. My entire body is tight and tense. My moans lengthen, becoming longer the closer I get. "Where does your husband come?"

"On my belly," I whisper.

"Have you ever been filled up?" he asks.

I swallow hard and shake my head. When Bryce fucked me, he didn't seem to savor being inside me. It was a place to push his frustration before dumping it onto my skin.

As Lex's pelvis grinds against my clit, with his cock deep inside me, I come. His hands travel down the curve of my spine and grip my ass.

"You're going to make me come, bunny." He fists my hair and cranes my neck so he can bite the skin of my throat. "I'm going to fill your pussy and then you're going to tell me if you want to live or die as my come drips from you."

I throb at his words, and it forces the pleasure from his cock. He comes inside me, the twitch of him deep in my gut. He stays within me instead of rushing away like Bryce. He basks in the pleasure I released from him, the pleasure he drew from me.

His hands ride up my sweaty body and grab both sides of my head once more. His touch makes me shiver. "What do you want?" he asks, his voice still laced with pleasure.

I had wanted to die, and even though that part of me still calls, another part has woken up and muffled its voice. I grab his hands and drag them away from my head. I wrap them within mine as I drop my chest into him, suddenly feeling twice as heavy. An exhausted pleasure weighs me down, but the weight of my sins also crushes me.

"Tell me what you want," he says.

"You," I whisper, accepting my sin.

And wanting more of it.

Chapter Seven

Lex

My mind remains on Selena as I drive us toward the next motel. We didn't get many miles under our belt because it was already late by the time I finished fucking her. It was everything I imagined, and I stayed inside her for as long as I could. As long as my dick cooperated. I had her hot, sweaty body pressed against mine, letting her cry into my chest until well past midnight. I wasn't the snuggling type—not in my nature—but I could have stayed there like that forever.

Once we get to the motel, I have no idea how she'll act toward me. She broke in front of my eyes, had asked me to do the unthinkable to her, and then came on my dick afterward. But on our drive to the motel, she hadn't given me any indication of how she felt. Was the sex only a moment in time where she felt empty and let me fill that void? Possibly.

Not that it can be anything more than that, anyway. I'm a dangerous hunter, and she's a sweet little rabbit.

I open the door to our room and go in before her. I flip

on the light, and it flickers above our heads. She looks around with much less disgust than before. I think she's getting used to being ripped from her luxury lifestyle and transplanted into motel rooms from hell. There's still no communication between us. It's a stale static that I'm sick of listening to.

She pushes past me to go into the bathroom, but I grab her arm and pull her back to me. Confusion muddies her eyes when she looks up at me. Her expression is racked with guilt, and it pisses me off more than it probably should.

"Why are you beating yourself up over what we did?" I ask as I shake her arm. She flinches from my touch. I'm not trying to hurt her, but I'll never understand why she cares so much about what we've done. People have had affairs in far less dire circumstances and never beat themselves up like this.

"Because I wasn't faithful to my husband." She's filled with regret and saturated in guilt.

"Get over it, rabbit." Her regret isn't my problem or responsibility. She knew what I would do to her, and she knows I won't feel bad about it. Not now. Not ever. I'm not sorry for fucking her, and I sure as hell don't regret giving her the strength to climb into that passenger seat and keep going.

"You don't understand," she whispers with a shake of her head.

I fist her hair. "I do understand. I've done a lot of shit I should regret. And maybe I even did for a minute. Don't tell me I don't understand the gravity of doing things I shouldn't. What do you think I'm running from?"

Tears gloss her eyes. "What are you serving life for?" she asks.

I nearly release her hair at that question. I didn't expect

it. I should have, but I forgot what she'd heard between Rodney and me. She found out more about me than she should have.

"Which life?" I say.

Her lip trembles. Yes, I'm serving multiple life sentences. My soul will be in prison for the next two life-times after this one. She has no idea what she let inside her, no idea who she let make her come. Twice.

"If you already regret fucking around on your piece of shit husband, don't ask me something like that when you know the answer will make you feel worse. Way fucking worse."

"I want to know. I deserve to know," she says with a defiant lift of her chin.

Who the hell does she think she is? She's out of her mind if she thinks she deserves anything more than the time she has left before we reach the end of the line.

She's lucky to get my cock in the interim.

I laugh, which makes her puff her chest. "Go on, rabbit." I push her toward the bathroom, but she digs her heels into the shitty carpet. "You keep your secrets, and I'll keep mine."

She flashes her eyes up at me. "Tell me yours, and I'll tell you mine."

Stupid girl. Yeah, her husband sounds like a controlling piece of shit, but she doesn't know what it's like to let the man who makes the devil blush sink into her pussy. When she hears what I've done, she'll just try to escape again. She'll probably puke from disgust when she finds out what kind of man she let inside her.

She swallows hard, and I stare at her throat as it bobs. "My husband beats me," she whispers.

"I know." I figured as much. I've seen glimpses of discoloration on her body. She isn't telling me some secret I didn't already piece together from her behavior. The things she's said. The fear on her face. The fact that he tracked her, for fuck's sake.

"No . . ." She shakes her head. Her gaze cuts away from mine as she raises her right sleeve, exposing bruises that are beginning to fade. It's hardly much to get upset about. It's not hard to bruise up a girl like her if you're rough enough, and it's easy to lose control. It's hard for *me* to avoid leaving marks on her.

Her lip trembles as she lifts the hem of her shirt, exposing some of the worst bruises I've ever seen on a living person. Her stomach and sides are shades of purple and pink. A yellow haze outlines anything that has begun to heal. *This* makes my heart quicken. Marks like that would have caused her a lot of pain. My mouth hangs open. I can't believe what I'm looking at. I can't believe how much it bothers me. It shouldn't. I shouldn't care.

But I do.

She has a way about her that makes me want to rip her away from all that hurt her so I can shield her under my own tattered wings.

"Goddamn it, Selena," I say through gritted teeth. I step into her and run my hand along her bruises. "How the fuck do you feel an ounce of guilt over what we did when he does *that* to you?"

She keeps her gaze locked on the floor and doesn't answer me. I force her to look at me by raising her chin. She looks ashamed.

"Don't pity me," she whispers, which is a really weird thing to fucking say, but not the weirdest thing she's said tonight.

"I don't pity you. I'm fucking pissed, though."

She trembles at the sharp rise in my voice. She looks like she fears I might hit her. I *am* mad, but not at her. I'm pissed at her piece of shit husband. I'm a bad fucking person, the worst of the worst, but I would never hurt her like this. I could never lay my hands on her like that, even if I've done worse to others.

I don't need to pity her, and she doesn't need anything from me. She'll gain her own wings, and then she won't need mine.

Against my better judgment, I decide to spill my guts to her, expose my underbelly and let her inside, even while knowing she won't like what she discovers within and that it will only push her away. She needs to know who she slept with.

I lean into her and get close to her ear. "Rabbit," I begin, "I'm a murderer. More than what you've seen tonight. I've killed innocent people. I killed my foster parents. I went to prison and killed fellow inmates. I'm a killer. It's what I've always been."

Her gasp pulls cool air over my skin. She fights the realization that she's let me inside her, a person so much worse than she imagined. Worse than anything she deserves.

A tear falls down her cheek and when I go to wipe it away, she rips away from my touch and runs into the bathroom, locking the door behind her. It's a fair response to finding out you came on the dick of a heartless killer.

Selena

OH GOD. Oh my fucking god. I pant against the door in a panic. In my heart I knew he was a killer when I saw him so casually choke out and then kill that man. As calm as watching a commercial on TV or mailing a letter. But I had no idea how much of a monster he was. Or that he'd killed so many. He's sick and twisted. A fucking psychopath.

And I'm stuck with him.

No wonder he was so willing to kill me. He's a seasoned killer. Realization pulls me under when I get the sick feeling that he plans to kill me at the end of this.

He has to. He can't let me go. I know his name. I know too much.

I get in the shower and let the hot water run over me, listening to the heavy tick of the invisible clock above my head. I should feel more fear and less acceptance about what I've realized, but if my time is limited, I'll make the best of what little is left. No matter which way the pendulum swings, death waits at both ends.

I wash up and get out of the shower. I slip the stiff towel around me, trying to hide the bruises beneath the rough terry cloth. When I step out of the bathroom, steam follows me. I carry my clothes in my hands. My eyes catch sight of my blouse and slacks folded on the dresser. I pick them up and sniff them. He must have washed them in the motel laundromat. Probably at the last shitty one.

He doesn't look at me as he walks past and goes into the bathroom to shower. I slip on my blouse and slacks, but then I remember what happened with my underwear. I curl my lip when I recall wearing my panties after he jerked off into them. He made me keep the saturated fabric against my pussy all night. He loved that little show of ownership and control. But he doesn't own me.

Asshole, I think as I pick up my clothes.

I'm not a fan of his, but I hate myself more for liking what I see when I look at him. For what I feel when I'm around him. I hate him for bringing out these feelings that rip me in two. One side tugs me toward being the good wife I was told to be in front of a room of people I hardly knew. The other side yanks me toward letting myself play with the lawless, and that side, like Lex, is stronger.

I get dressed and lie in the single bed. I push the stained cover toward my feet. The sheet beneath it looks clean enough, at least. I curl up in bed, my dark, wet hair soaking the off-white pillowcase beneath my head. I stare straight ahead at the peeling paint on the wall . . . until I hear the bathroom door slam.

Lex is naked. I pretend to be asleep, but I peek at the cords of muscles in his arms. He has a prisoner's body—the type of physique a convict attains when there is nothing else to do but work out. His damp hair is brushed back. His taut back muscles connect to one of the most perfect asses I've ever seen on a man. I wish I had gotten to see how a body that perfect would have merged with mine. Perfect versus the most imperfect. Regret at that longing immediately fills me.

He's a killer, I remind myself.

I squeeze my eyes closed as he turns around. I'm not in the right frame of mind to talk about anything more tonight. I'm drained, overwhelmed, and more tired than I've ever been in my life.

Lex gets into bed beside me, tugging up the disgusting blanket I'd kicked away. When he turns over and backs into me, I realize his back and ass are bare. And against me. I can't believe he got into bed naked with me. I try to scoot over an inch, but I meet the edge of the mattress. My eyes clench shut, and I hope he doesn't notice the change in my breathing. I'm worried he'll feel the discomfort radiating from me as I draw my arms against my body.

"It's just nudity, rabbit. Don't get your panties in a bunch," he says without turning over.

His words infuriate me. I scoff. "I don't have panties to get in a bunch, thanks to you." I draw my legs toward my chest, making myself as small as I can.

He laughs. He fucking laughs. "Oh yeah, that's right."

His body stills as he sobers. He never tries to turn toward me. He allows the gap of space between me and his naked body. "Goodnight, bunny," he whispers before silence falls between us.

Chapter Eight

Lex

I wake up the same way I went to sleep, except now a cold sweat coats my body. The alarm clock by the bed buzzes like a hive of angry bees. The time on the clock is only a few hours later. Nothing is worse than waking up restless next to a goddamn woman like her. Actually, next to any woman at all, but she's especially difficult to just exist beside.

I turn onto my back and stare up at the dark ceiling. Every so often, headlights illuminate the room through the thin veil of the inner curtains. For a while I worried about her husband finding us, but as the days passed without him sending the goddamn army to find her, I can't help but wonder if he even cared that she was gone. Not just about being married or the marriage-centric image he portrayed, but actually cared about *her*. Is she safe? Dead? With all that generational wealth he has, why isn't he doing everything he can to get his girl back? A girl like her would make me do some real fucked-up shit to find her and bring her home.

She stirs beside me, and I hold my breath for a moment until she settles. She's making me anxious. I feel guilt and regret and something else that I can't put my finger on. I hate knowing I'll have to kill her when we get to Texas, but it's better than sending her home to the piece of shit who bruised her abdomen like that. I can't bring her with me, not that someone like her would come along anyway. Life on the run wouldn't work for a girl like her. There aren't any spas or fancy new cars on the lam.

My mind wanders to how I imagine her husband looks. Probably nothing like me. Probably well dressed and put together. Someone her parents love more than she does. All I know for sure is that he's a little-dicked piece of shit who likes to beat up on his woman.

The irony isn't lost on me. I never treated women much better, and I'd be lying if I called myself any kind of saint. She's *different*, though, and I can't wrap my mind around his inability to see that. How can he not when it's so disgustingly clear to me? With everything else good in his life, he also has her beneath him.

Fucking idiot.

My cock hardens at the thought of him fucking her. It shouldn't, but it does. I recognize the appearance of the side of me that wants to see that. A familiar to me—yet foreign to her—entity that occasionally screams in my head. At times, that side of me is hard to disregard.

I ache with an uncomfortable throb I can't ignore. My hand slips to my cock, and I bite the inside of my cheek as I wrap my fingers around the head of my dick. I circle myself with my fist as I try to be quiet and still, like I had to do when I was on the inside. I was polite about it, at least, unlike some of my roommates who jerked it loud enough to wake up the whole row.

I bite back a groan. Fuck, I want her. I *need* her. Never in my life have I wanted to rip the clothes from a woman so completely.

At this moment, with my head in all the wrong places, I turn over and scoot closer to her back. She remains motionless as I press my hard cock against her ass. There's no way she doesn't feel it. I run my hand down her side, knowing there are bruises beneath my touch. If she doesn't feel my dick pressed against her, she'll feel that.

"Don't pretend to sleep, bunny," I whisper.

She tenses and tries to fake a heavy sleep as my hand reaches the waistband of her pants and travels to the front of her slacks. I unbutton them and lower the zipper. I reach into the newly splayed fabric, rubbing the soft skin of her lower stomach and the soft hairs of her pelvis.

"There's no way you don't feel this," I say in a hushed tone as I tug her pants down. "Being asleep doesn't make it any less wrong, you know? Pretending to be asleep doesn't make it any less sinful."

I pull her pants past her ass and push my cock between her thighs. I groan at the warmth of her pussy against me. I grip my cock and guide myself into her. The muscles inside her twitch at the intrusion, and the tension rides up her entire body. She's still trying to remain faithful. It's a pathetic and sad attempt to fight what she wants and what I need. What we both need. She's too fucking wet to pretend she doesn't want it, too.

"Goddamn it, rabbit," I groan as I draw my hips back and slam them into her. It's too dark to see her face and gauge her reaction. I hope a pair of headlights will cross the window so I can see her open eyes. Because I know she's awake. "You're being childish," I say through gritted teeth. I get sick of it. I refuse to play the fucked-up game she made up to avoid the reality we're in. To avoid letting me in.

I sink my fingers into the worst of her bruises, and she yelps. Finally, a fucking reaction. I roll her onto her stomach and keep my cock deep inside her as I press her face into the pillow. Her legs clench together beneath me, and the friction is enough to make me want to bust.

"Lex . . ."

I push my hips forward, going deeper inside her. "Good morning, bunny," I say with a growl as I wipe the hair from her cheek.

"You're . . . hurting me," she whispers.

"I'm not even doing anything to hurt you . . . yet."

As she pants, pain weaves through every breath. She's wet, stretching around me just right. I'm not hurting her pussy. Not like that, at least.

"Get off me . . . please," she begs.

Despite how fucking good she feels around my cock and how much I don't want to pull out of her, I do. Self-restraint has never been a strong skill of mine, so I struggle between the bit of humanity she draws out of me versus everything I've always been.

I get out of bed, snatch the sheet around me, and flip the light switch, illuminating the room. She's pulled up her pants, but they're still undone.

"What the hell is the matter with you?" I ask, harsher than I intend, even though her wetness coating my cock makes me *almost* too hungry to stay off her.

"I—" she begins, but the rest of the words are choked off. Her lip trembles, and she cuts her gaze from mine. Her body shakes, and that broken little girl is suddenly back in front of me.

I sigh, wiping a hand through my hair. I gather my composure as best I can and walk to her side of the bed, a hand still clutching the white sheet around my waist. I lift her chin with the other, forcing her to look at me. "What was hurting you?" I ask again, more forcefully this time. "It wasn't my cock, so what was it?"

"The bruises," she whispers.

"On your stomach?" When I rolled her onto her stomach, I was careful with her. I tried to be, at least.

She shakes her head.

"There's more?" I ask, but I know the answer already. There must be more marks on her skin than what she showed me. I force her to her feet, and she flinches when I grip her bruised wrist. "Show me," I command. I leave no room for argument.

When I reach out for the buttons on the front of her blouse, she screams out a no that *almost* makes me stop. I bat her hand away and return to the buttons. She keeps wiggling and fighting me. I release my hold on the sheet, and it falls to my feet as I knock her back into the nightstand. The lamp teeters behind her. I grab her arms and pin them to her sides, and she releases a whimper.

"Stop fighting me," I seethe.

"Please don't," she begs. Her eyes widen with fear, as if she thinks I'll hate her once I see what waits beneath her clothes. Or at least think differently of her. Her hands go for my wrists again.

"If you don't keep your hands at your fucking sides, Selena, I'm going to grab my gun, put it up to your pretty little head, and force you to strip for me. Your choice." She's gnawing on my last nerve.

Her hands finally fall to her sides and remain there. I work the buttons off, one by one. She keeps her face turned away from me as the fabric spreads on her chest. More bruises. They cover her sternum and wash down her breasts. I can't even take a moment to enjoy her tits because I can't believe what I am seeing.

The front of her pants is still undone, but I ignore the brown hair between her legs and focus on another patch of purple peeking from beneath the fabric. I reach for her waistband, and she grabs my wrists with undeniable fear on her face. She's forgotten the threat I made because what I'm doing is scarier than my gun.

"Leave my pants on," she pleads.

Absolutely not.

"No, Selena. I'm going to see every inch of you. I need to know where you're hurt."

Tears fall down her cheeks, an uncontrolled overflow of her emotional pain. I slide her slacks down and my mouth gapes. More bruises. The worst is a large mark that takes up the entire length of her outer left thigh. I'm guessing that's what hurt her when I pinned her beneath my weight. My knee dug into that area, keeping her legs together as I pushed deeper inside her. Or it may have been her chest, where her hands would have been pinned beneath her breasts.

"Oh, bunny," I whisper as I rub my hand up her thigh, making her nearly jump from the pain. I wonder how I didn't hurt her in the car, but then I remembered that leg would have been cushioned against the back seat when I was over her. It all makes sense.

My erection is gone, and I hang limp between my legs. She cries as she tries to cover herself again. She looks ashamed more than anything, which rubs me in all the wrong ways. Shame isn't what she should feel. Her fucking husband should carry this burden, not her.

"I'm usually fine with pain," she rationalizes as she buttons her pants with trembling fingers. "I'm used to it. But your knee pressed right into this bruise"—she touches her left thigh—"and it was too much."

When she goes to take a breath to keep babbling on, I take the chance to pull her into my chest. She swallows the words instead of continuing. My heart breaks for her, and I don't understand how it can when I've never had one. I've never felt sympathy for anyone or anything. But my blame shifts in my selfish mind. If she hadn't tried to play Sleeping Beauty, I wouldn't have pinned her like that. I curse myself for putting the blame back on her. I'm the one who was too forceful.

"Sweet bunny," I whisper, "I'm going to fuck you, and then we're going back to New York."

She looks up at me and tries to wipe the tears from her cheeks. "But . . . why?"

I brush her hair from her face. It's sticky with the salt of her tears. "Because I'm going to kill your fucking husband."

She shakes her head. "We can't."

I fist her hair. "Which part?"

Instead of answering, she drops her jaw and allows her lower lip to tremble.

"Sweet little rabbit," I growl, "I can answer that for you. Of course I can fuck you. I was just inside you. And since I'm a murderer, I can kill your husband for putting these bruises on you." My fingers trace her chest, only partially concealed by her blouse. I drop a hand between her thighs and move upward, past the bruises that make her flinch.

"We can't kill him."

I lean closer to her mouth. "*We* aren't going to. *You* aren't doing anything. I'll take care of everything, just like I'll take care of you." I kiss her, and her breath hitches as I tug down her pants. She slips out of them, and I look at her. Fully look at her.

She's naked except for the white blouse covering her nipples. I see every bruise. Her brokenness makes me feel like I need to mend her instead of being the one who does more of the breaking. I remove the last bit of fabric hiding her body from me, and she drops her gaze.

"Don't be embarrassed about your body. These marks don't shame you. They shame *him*. Your piece of shit husband."

She flinches at the word *husband*, and my eyes narrow.

"Goddamn it, rabbit! Stop fucking caring about him. He doesn't care about you."

"But—"

"But nothing." I turn her around and pull her closer. I run a rough hand down the big bruise on her left thigh, and she jolts. "This isn't from a man who cares."

She scoffs. "Abducting a woman at gunpoint is A-okay to you, though? What do you call that?"

I bite the sensitive skin of her shoulder. My cock hardens against her ass. "Desperation? Your lucky day?" I say with a smirk as I kiss where I bit her, and I swear I see a hint of a smile cross her face.

I carefully wrap my arm around her waist, trying to avoid the bruises on her stomach as I bend her over the bed. When her elbows hit the mattress, only the mark on her wrist has pressure against it. No pain.

I run my hands down her sides, tracing the bruises that wrap around and lick at her back. Her ass somehow remains pale and perfect, without a mark on it. I want to change that so goddamn bad, but she needs to stay unmarked . . . for now. I need to give her pleasure as I show her what it's like to have a real man inside her. A man who is as angry and violent as I am, yet still wouldn't hit her.

"Lex," she whispers. There's a hint of longing in the word, a desire I've been desperate to hear.

"What do you want?" I growl. "Use your words. You know I like that."

"I want you inside me."

"Inside what? In your ass? Your pussy?"

"My . . . pussy."

"Good girl."

I fist her hair, grip my cock, and push inside her. She whimpers as she drops her head and rests it on her fists. She feels incredible. And she looks amazing. I lean over her and run my hand down her stomach until I reach the dripping excitement between her legs.

"Goddamn it, bunny," I groan as I move my fingers along the seam of her pussy. Her clit swells beneath my touch. I rub her until she backs into me to take my cock deeper. I lift her to me, wrapping my free arm around her chest. "Your husband is so fucking stupid. You know that, right?"

She hesitates for a moment before whimpering out a yes.

"I'm going to fuck you in your bed at home. Make him watch. I want him to look at what he lost until his very last breath."

Her cheeks flush. "Lex . . . don't talk about him."

I laugh. "Until he's dead, I'll mention him as I fuck you."

She tightens her lips, but they spread again as I rub circles over her clit. I caress her most sensitive area until she moans—a sound I love to hear.

"Come for me," I command as I bite her neck. "Be a good little bunny and come."

She squeezes around me, choking my dick, and I fight against her body to stay deep inside her. I rub her until she shudders against my grasp on her chest. As she spasms, her body coming down from the violent twitches of her orgasm, I thrum my thumb back and forth over her clit.

"Lexington," she whispers.

I hate my full name because it's the name on every form, every newspaper, blasted all over the internet. I hate when people call me Lexington because when they do, it calls to *him,* the person I'm trying not to be around her. It calls to the side of me I despise. The part of me who thinks about her and her husband together. The part of me I don't want to let out to play with her.

I hate that name, but when it falls from her parted lips that way, I love it.

The moment we get to Texas, I'll be off her hands—out of her hair and out of her pussy. I fully intended to kill her, eliminating any chance for her to offer information to the law regarding my whereabouts. But now?

I've decided I'll set the rabbit free.

Chapter Nine

Selena

I couldn't believe he meant what he said last night when he mentioned returning to New York. I thought he'd change his mind or that he'd said it just to sleep with me. I didn't think he'd turn around when we were so close to his freedom. I didn't expect him to go back for anything, not even to get his hands on Bryce. He isn't worth getting caught over, and if Lex gets caught, I'll end up alone with the true monster: my husband.

I watch Lex from the passenger seat as he drives. Every so often he shoots a look over at me and flashes a quick smirk.

"We should go back," I say with a nervous shake of my knee beside the center console.

He raises an eyebrow. "We *are* going back."

I scoff. "You know what I mean. Back the way we were going. Away from here."

"Rabbit, stop," he says with a stern tone that makes me

shut my mouth. "If you're going to be mouthy, use it in a better way."

My jaw drops at his brazen words. He talks to me like I'm his whore, a toy to use. And now, with him, I want to be played with like that. My eyes land on the hard dick beneath the zipper of his jeans. My leg stops shaking as I stare at him.

He reaches out and grabs my hand, caressing my palm. "Did you stroke your husband's dick?"

I nod, keeping my eyes on him.

"Show me how." He brings my hand to the zipper. I consider arguing—believe me, I consider it—but an aching in my gut keeps my hand in place.

The denim scrapes against the soft pads of my fingers as I drag them toward the button. I swallow hard, lean over, and work open his pants. He isn't wearing boxers, giving me a glimpse of his cock.

"Don't be shy. You've seen it all already," he says as he fully reveals his cock, sick of me taking my time to expose him. His hand rides along his shaft before circling his head and planting itself on the steering wheel again. I stare at the bead of pre-cum on his head and feel guilt the moment it drips over the curve.

I dig my fingers into his jeans. He's already been inside me—twice. He already made me come—three times. Stroking his dick hardly seems like it'll matter at this point. I can just add it to my list of sins.

I draw a deep breath before wrapping my hand around the hot skin.

"Good girl," he groans. His fingers dig into the steering wheel as I stroke him. Despite the soft buck of his hips, he keeps the car steady on the road, which is much better than I did. "I need your mouth, bunny," he says through a groan.

I shake my head. "Wh-what? I can't. You're driving."

"So? Get on your knees and lean over my lap."

I shake my head.

"Now, rabbit! Don't make me ask you again. You can suck me off your way or my way, your choice."

I hate when he gives choices. They're never good ones.

I swallow the lump in my throat and undo my seatbelt. I swivel my head, looking at the quiet, empty road.

"Fine," I say as I climb onto my knees.

As I lean over his lap, he grabs my hair, lifting it away from my face and bunching it in his hand. I take him into my mouth. He groans in a way that shakes his whole body, like I've sent a shockwave through him. I suck him, and his hips pulse toward my mouth, forcing me to take more of him. His hand leaves my hair and plants on my ass. His fingers graze my lower back as his hand returns to my hair. He pulls me off his dick, and I look up at him.

"Does he make you suck his cock?" he asks.

I nod.

"Was he the first man you put your mouth on?"

I give him another nod, straining against his grasp. He just smirks at me as he pushes me down on his dick. He groans when my tongue meets his skin again.

"Sweet bunny, you have the best mouth I've ever felt."

His cock impales the back of my throat when he thrusts his hips upward, which makes me gag. A deep growl leaves Lex's lips. Tears slip from my eyes as I pull back enough to keep from throwing up, and I take some quick breaths through my nose before he pushes me to the base of his cock. I gag again, but he holds me there to keep me from pulling away this time. My throat tightens, and I use my lips to protect his warm skin from my teeth. My whole body shudders. He lets go so I can draw a breath without my nose buried in skin and hair.

"God, I love how you choke on my dick. Is your husband as big as me? Has he ever made you gag like this?"

I pull away from his cock and shake my head. Bryce wasn't big at all, thank God. He'd have used it as a weapon if he was as blessed as Lex.

He wipes the tears from my cheek and licks the salty evidence of what he does to me. He moans and pulls me up to kiss him, making me taste my tears as well. He fists my hair harder, and I see the glimpse of cars driving past as he pulls me back toward his lap. The other drivers can see me, ass up and doing what I'm doing, and my cheeks flush with embarrassment. The tip of his cock touches my lips.

"People can see me," I whine against him.

"Good. You're a fancy little show rabbit. You should be shown off," he growls before shoving me back down. "If you keep taking your mouth off me, I'll make you get on my lap and ride my dick. Your choice." He lifts his hips and pushes his cock to the back of my throat. I choke out air. "Good girl," he whispers. "Slip your hand down your pants and play with yourself."

I try to pull back to speak, but he holds me in place.

"Remember what I said," he tells me through a tense jaw.

I have no choice but to listen to him. My hand wanders down the front of my leggings, and I'm surprised by how wet I am. This isn't really the type of thing that gets me going, but there *is* something about the way he reacts to my touch and the feeling of my tongue riding along the perfect curve of his cock that excites me.

I rub two fingers along my slit. He controls the speed of my head as I control what happens between my legs. My moans vibrate against his cock, and the feral groan he releases vibrates against *me*. As I get closer to my edge, I feel the need to pull him from my mouth. The tense muscles in my body make it harder to keep my teeth off him.

"Is it too much for you? Having trouble keeping those teeth off my dick? You can bite, sweet bunny. You can't hurt me."

I shake my head as best I can.

"Fine. Take your mouth off me so you can come, but don't you dare stop stroking."

I pull him from my mouth and pant as I wrap my hand around him and keep stroking his cock. He's still wet from my spit. With his hand wound through my hair, he brings my face to his and kisses me, hard. His eyes watch the road as his mouth moves against mine, pushing me over the edge.

"Come for me, bunny," he groans.

And I do. I come so fucking hard, dropping my weight into him and making him swerve.

"That good?" he asks with a smirk.

"Fuck off," I say with a pleasure-laced laugh.

Lex's eyebrow rises. "I wanted to come inside you again, but I was trying to be amenable and settle for your throat. Not gonna work. I need your pussy."

My lower jaw drops, and I shake my head. Absolutely no way in hell am I riding his dick while going seventy miles per hour down the highway.

Lex leans over and hits the bar to push the seat back.

"I'm not doing that," I say.

"Rabbit," he says firmly, and the ice in his tone forces me to reconsider. "Take your pants off."

There's that voice again—the voice that makes me weak because it's so strong.

I stare at him, trying to ignore the thunder of my heart

roaring in my ears. I hook my fingers into the waistband of my leggings and tug them down. I'm a sticky, wet mess from my own come.

"Climb onto my lap." He taps his thigh.

I swallow hard, surveying the road once more before carefully climbing in front of him, trying not to hit the steering wheel as I stare out the windshield. He drops one hand and helps me onto his lap. He grips my hip, sinks inside me, and lets out a growl that sends a shiver down my spine, right to the notch of the hip he's holding. He takes his other hand off the steering wheel and grabs my other hip.

"Drive," he says with a groan. "If I try to drive while buried in your perfect cunt like this, I'm liable to kill us both." His teeth scrape my shoulder before he bites into my neck. "I'm not going to last long with you. Your pussy is so fucking wet. All from my cock, huh?"

"Yes," I whimper, and try to keep my eyes on the road and my hands on the wheel as he thrusts against me. He's so fucking deep, and it makes it hard to keep the car on a straight path.

"I'm going to come," he whispers. His hips pulse before settling beneath me. I make a move to get off his lap, but he holds me in place. "Not yet, sweet bunny." He slips his hands from my hips to the wheel in front of me. "I want to feel you around me for a little while longer."

I sigh and drop back against his chest as he drives. His cock twitches inside me, and I stop caring about the occasional car that drives by as I sit on the heat of his cock. He kisses the top of my head, which almost doesn't feel real.

He doesn't seem like the sweet type. But then again, this isn't who I am, either.

Chapter Ten

Lex

I'm being incredibly fucking dumb over some woman who wouldn't have given me the time of day had I not forced her. I'm wanted. Every law enforcement agency in New York is actively seeking me out, and yet here I am, driving back into the heart of their search. I'm taking a huge risk by bringing us back here, but I can't let her go home to *him*. I have to protect her, even if she's not with me.

Especially if she's not with me.

I'm not sure how she feels about everything. If she thinks I'm kidding when I say I plan on killing her husband, she's in for a big surprise. I'll get rid of that piece of shit and when we get to Texas, I can leave while knowing she'll be safe.

When have I ever given a shit about someone's safety aside from my own? Never. Old me would have wished her good fucking luck and let her go home to that shitbag. Or I would have just killed her. Either way, this selfless behavior is very new to me.

We drive past darkness. I turn off at an exit, which piques Selena's interest.

"Where are we going?" she asks. Her voice is heavy with exhaustion. We're both tired. I can't drive anymore, and neither should she.

"I want to show you something. And besides, motels in this state would be too risky."

We drive down a road dense with trees on both sides, and I pull to the side of the asphalt, concealing the car among the overgrown bushes before I cut the engine. I get out of the car, open her door, and offer her my hand. She stares at me.

"Come on, rabbit."

She draws a sharp breath before taking my hand and getting out of the car.

Crickets chirp and break the quiet. There's little to see except for lightning bugs blinking between the trees. She wraps her arms around herself. I'm not sure if it's from fear of the dark or what. She should know by now I would protect her, even if I'm the one who drags her toward danger in the first place.

"You're okay," I tell her, though I feel her gaze burn through me.

When we get to the end of the path, I leap onto the rocks and reach down for her. She sighs and puts her hand in mine as I help her up. A sharp gasp leaves her lips the moment her feet hit the stone beneath her.

We overlook the town below. Lights on every building dot the landscape. It looks surreal. Like how I remembered, but better, because Selena is here to enjoy it with me.

"What is this place?"

I swallow hard. "Someplace I used to go when I was

younger. A safe place when my foster parents were being extra shitty."

I sit at the edge of the cliff, dangling my legs over. Dirt falls from the soles of my shoes. "Come sit," I say. She walks over and squats down to brush off the grass. I cock my head at her. "Even fancy show rabbits get dirty." I tug her down beside me, and she plops onto the grass with a huff. I hate that look on her face. The judgment.

She clears her throat. "I'm not used to—"

"Getting your designer jeans dirty?" I ask with an annoyed snap in my tone.

She shakes her head. "That's not what I meant." She sighs. "I'm not used to being free."

Oh. "Me neither." I lie back, dropping my head onto my hands. My shirt rises and I feel true freedom against my skin as the wind races over us.

The moon illuminates her silhouette, and I take a deep breath. She feels so right to be around. She almost feels like a friend. It's as close to having a friend as I've ever known, anyway. But I know it's all pretend, and that makes me sort of . . . sad. I didn't get sad when I was sentenced to life, sentenced again, and then once more. I can't remember ever feeling sad like this. I turned that emotion off at a very young age. I had to. I wouldn't have survived if I let myself feel anything but anger and hatred for myself or anyone else.

"Lay with me, bunny," I whisper as I grab her shoulder and pull her into me. As if she has a choice. She tenses before relaxing into me.

Silence blankets us, except for the sound of nature. That's something I haven't listened to in over a decade. I close my eyes and bathe in it. Listening to something other than the hoot and holler of fellow inmates is fucking incredible.

Selena shivers, and I sit up enough to shimmy out of my long-sleeved shirt and offer it to her. She hesitates before she takes it and slips it on. I lie back, not giving a shit about the scratchy grass beneath my bare skin because at least I can feel it instead of the rough mattress in my cell.

She traces my tattoos, or what she can see of them under the light of the moon. I'm not proud of all of them, and I'm thankful she doesn't ask about them as her finger-tips glide along my skin. I didn't hang out with the best crowds on the inside. Not that any of us could be considered the best crowd.

Her hand falls away, and soft snores come from beside me. The way she's snuggled up to me feels fucking weird. I've always been alone, especially in prison. In there, loneliness was a godsend. Growing up, I had to be okay with being alone because being lonely meant I wasn't having the shit beat out of me by the man paid to care for me.

I close my eyes. "Goodnight, bunny," I whisper as I let myself drift into sleep.

Selena

I WAKE up to a shiver of cold morning air racing over my cheek. Cool dew wets my skin. Birds chirp from somewhere nearby. I look around, trying to orient myself. I'm on Lex's arm, which is insane. He's shirtless and I'm wearing his shirt. He gave it to me when I was cold. He's such a walking contradiction. He looks almost . . . sweet. Serene.

"Morning," he says as he opens his blue eyes. His skin pebbles with morning chill. He leans over and wraps a strong arm around me, but I push him away. We aren't going to cuddle like this. We can't.

He takes no offense to my shrugging him off as he sits up, pulls his arm from under me, and gets to his feet. He puts his hand down and smirks. "Come, rabbit," he whispers.

I grab his hand and stand on legs that feel heavy. I'm stiff from having slept outside on the cool ground. We walk toward the car, but he pulls me to the right before it comes into view.

"Lex, the car's that way." I point back the way we came.

"Excellent observation."

"Where are we going?"

"Do you trust me?" he asks as I dig my heels into the ground.

"Not really, no."

He looks back at me and chuckles.

The trees open up and expose a large pond. The early sunlight reflects off the dark water. Ripples drift across the surface with every puff of breeze, and a small bird struts along the opposite bank, pecking here and there for its breakfast.

I stare as Lex unties his shoes and slips off his socks. He unbuttons and unzips his jeans and lets the fabric spread, exposing the soft, light hair on his pelvis. My mouth gapes as he tugs off his jeans. His cock is limp, hanging low against his thigh, but the flood of memories from him being hard rip through me, heating my body.

"Your turn," he says with a flirty grin.

"Wh-what? No. I'm not swimming in that," I tell him, as if I have any say in the matter.

"Get undressed, rabbit, or I'll come do it for you."

I pout. Childish, yes, but I do *not* want to go in that water.

When I still don't remove my clothes, he steps closer and makes good on his threat. He strips me until I'm naked in front of him. His cock is now hard and pressed against my lower belly.

"Why must you always fight me? You're the little bunny, and I'm the coyote. I'll always win."

I stare at him, my lower lip trembling in time with the rest of my body. My skin freezes, and not even the sun is enough to warm it. He grabs me, pressing his hard dick against my lower back as I flail. He carries me to the pond and throws me in. I scream until my head submerges, and I continue to scream the moment I resurface. The water isn't as cold as I expected, and it doesn't choke the air from my lungs. It's almost refreshing, but still, fuck him.

"Fuck you, Lex!"

He smirks and jumps in after me. When he surfaces, he tosses his head, his hair rushing back. Water drips from his nose and lips, and he looks so handsome at this moment. I hate how much I want to take in all his soaked and naked features and commit them to memory. He looks like he was carved by the devil himself.

I kick my feet to keep my head above water while he just stands. He's annoying like that. He moves closer and wraps me up in his arms. I steady my legs and float there as he holds me.

"Rabbits don't like to swim, huh?" he says as he curls my legs around his waist.

"Not by force."

"All of this has been by force," he says with a smirk. Lex

brushes the hair away from my face. "You swam just fine so far."

My heart thrums against my chest. The sun blazes down on my pale shoulders. The world melts around us, dripping down like the water off our naked bodies.

"What do you want, sweet bunny?" he whispers. I didn't realize I was staring so hard at his lips until he spoke. His words paint the landscape again, dotting it with trees. His finger rides along my pouty lower lip. "If you want a kiss, you need to take it."

I won't kiss him. It still feels too wrong. Even though he's made me come, it wasn't initiated by *me*. I can still hold on to that stupid fact. I pretend my refusal to initiate means I've somehow negated the copious amount of infidelity we've already engaged in.

Even though my thoughts are unfaithful.

"You're so fucking stubborn," he says when I don't make a move. His hand wraps around the back of my neck and pulls me into him. He kisses me, and I let him. A frustrated groan leaves his cold, wet lips. "I'm going to take you back to the car, lay you down on the hood, and fuck you with my mouth."

No one has ever talked to me like that. It's exciting and equally terrifying. I can count on one hand the number of times Bryce has gone down on me, and I remember the stale movement of his jaw as he did. It seemed like a chore to him. I have a feeling Lex will eat me like I'm his last meal before going to his death. He'll walk to his execution with a belly full of every moment since we met. He'll leave me feeling devoured, never happy with the feasting of any other man. And he knows it as his hand rides up the back of my thighs and grabs my ass.

I push away from him and start to swim across the pond, kicking my feet as I tread water with my hands. The thought turns me on and pokes at a playful side of me I didn't know I had. I've probably always had that side, but I've never been allowed to let it surface until now, in the freedom of a serene pond with a man like Lex.

"Where are you going?" he calls.

"Catch me if you can, predator." I let out a chuckle.

He growls and takes off after me as I swim away from shore. Once the pond gets too deep, he swims toward me, his muscular body cutting through the water like a bullet. I hold my breath, dive under, and propel myself beneath the cool surface. Sounds are muffled, and a suffocating silence surrounds me. I open my eyes and take in the greens and browns on every side of me. I can't hear him or feel a change in the water, but I know he's there, hot on my trail. I feel his breath on my neck, even when I know it's not possible.

When my lungs beg for air, I pop up to take a quick and hearty breath. I can't see him. Ripples of the disrupted water roll away from me. As I turn to swim toward shore, I hear him surface behind me.

"Sneaky little prey," he says. I don't need to turn around to know his eyes have taken on a darker cast. I hear it in his voice. It's a visceral hunger lurking just below the surface that chills my veins and tells me this is no longer fun and games. When he catches me, he'll devour me.

I kick my legs and push myself toward the shore. I have to swim long after he can walk, but I still make it first. Barely. The rocky bottom scrapes my knees as I try to get to my feet and run from him. I can't look back because he's only steps behind me.

Grass cushions my bare feet, pine needles cling to my wet ankles, and I can hear his heavy, dedicated footsteps closing in. They thunder in my ears and compete with my heartbeat. I have no choice but to leave my clothes behind as I take off toward the car.

My heart nearly beats from my chest, ready to rip through my sternum. I instigated the chase and now I'm the one feeling hunted. Afraid. But I should be. I picked a true predator to chase me—to hunt me like the little rabbit he thinks I am. It's all so fucking dumb. The moment he gets his hands on me, I'm in for it. No amount of pleading will stop him from taking what he wants. What he captured. What he worked up a sweat for.

I touch my car's silver hood. It's hot from the sun's early rays. Just as my fingers land on the hot metal, strong arms grab me. He pants against my ear; it's the worst frustration I've ever seen. Like a predator who chased his prey, only to have it pivot at the last moment and escape his mighty jaws. Only . . . I didn't escape, and I won't be able to now.

He's trying to hold back and stay in control. I feel it in the tremble of the muscles in his strong body. Lex growls as he turns me around and pushes me against the hood of my car. He lifts me and lays me on my back. He has me in his grasp and doesn't look like he has any intention of letting me go. Pieces of his slicked-back hair fall over his forehead, and he brushes them back with a frustrated motion.

"That was really stupid, rabbit." He's so close to my mouth I feel every syllable against my lips.

I know it was stupid. He doesn't need to remind me. I have no clue why I did it. I just did, and now I'm in the clutches of the most dangerous predator I've ever met. He's not a coyote. He's a wolf. A majestic and beautiful creature that would happily tear me to shreds.

"I want to rip through you, take you," he groans. "But I'm trying . . . really trying . . . to make you feel good instead." The metal burns me as he yanks me toward him and lifts my thighs. I try to keep them closed, but he rips them apart with a rough touch. His fingers make the bruises on my thighs ache, and when I flinch, he ignores the pain and holds them open.

"Don't you close those legs. I told you I would lay you on this goddamn hood and fuck you with my mouth."

And he does. Oh god, he fucking does. He buries his face between my legs and licks at me like he's ripping the flesh off my bones with his tongue. It's rough enough that I raise my hips to put some space between my pussy and his mouth. He releases one of my thighs and puts a flat hand on my pelvis, pushing me against the metal.

"Don't you move away from me. Stay here and let me take what I caught." He looks up at me from between my legs. "Don't start a game you can't handle losing."

I shiver at his words, and he buries his face into me again. He keeps me firmly planted against the metal. His teeth rake the hood of my clit between him sucking on it, and it's like nothing I've ever felt—an uncomfortable pain and pleasure fighting for survival within me.

"Lex," I whisper.

He doesn't respond, just shoves three of his fingers inside me. I scream out as he stretches me. It's too sudden. I wasn't ready for it. I'm not ready for any part of him.

I never will be.

With his fingers deep inside me, he starts to lick me again. "I love it when you moan, bunny," he whispers against my clit. "It shows me you've forgotten you're married for a few minutes. Forgotten I'm the bad guy and that you let me make you come." He growls and dips his tongue inside me before pulling out and running it over my clit in a long stroke.

I bury my hand in his hair and tug him toward me, unable to resist the growing pleasure between my legs.

He pulls away from me. "I'd tell you to get your hand off me, but I want to feel you force my mouth into your pussy when you come."

I tremble at his whispered words.

His fingers push deeper inside me, and my warm wetness slips past them. He fucks me with his fingers while he works me with his tongue until I spasm around him. My chest rises, lifting my back from the hood of the car. I ride out my orgasm with a few long licks of his tongue that leave me bucking my hips against his mouth with every intense sensation.

He pulls me off the hood of my car, the metal scraping my sweat-coated skin. He turns me around, puts my hands on the hood, and drops to his knees. Before I can even get a word out, his tongue moves across my slit and keeps rising upward. I gasp as he reaches the only place on me he hasn't put his mouth.

Oh God, we are not doing *that*.

I try to pull away from him, but he grabs my hips and holds me back.

"No, Lex," I say firmly. Even as his tongue starts to feel good there. Different.

"Shh, rabbit. When I eat you, I want to devour *all* of you. Prey doesn't question how they're being eaten, they just let the predator get its fill."

He licks me and I surprise myself when a moan leaves my lips. This is wrong. It feels so damn wrong. But why does it also feel good? Dirty? Rugged? Like the man behind me.

"Every bit of you tastes like a delicacy I shouldn't get to eat. Something much too fancy for me."

"Lex," I say through a moan, and reach back to grip his hair. I surprise myself once more when it's not to pull him away but to keep him there.

He pushes his fingers inside my pussy, and I'm overwhelmed by the sensations all over again. He fucks me with his fingers and licks me until I find myself teetering on another edge I never expected.

One I've never known.

I drop my free hand back to the hood and steady myself as he brings me toward another orgasm. "Fuck," I moan, and he gives me a hard thrust in response. His fingers pull out of me to rub my clit, circling until he's over it, thrumming my hood directly. It's a sensation that instantly kicks me over the edge, like a pulse of electricity with every swipe of his thumb.

I drop both hands to the hood. My thighs tremble, and I struggle to stay on my feet. He spanks my clit as I ride the coattails of my orgasm with a whimper.

"Naughty mouth on you," he says through a laugh as he slips his tongue back in his mouth and stands up. He wipes at his chin, which is coated in my come. "I knew you'd like that, dirty little rabbit. I bet your husband has *never* eaten you like that."

I look up at him, a hint of fear crawling over me when I recognize the darkness in his gaze. He wraps his hand around the front of my throat and squeezes.

For a moment I wonder if this is it. If he's going to kill me.

"Get your clothes and get in the fucking car," he snarls, and loosens his grasp on my neck.

"What'd I do?" I ask.

"You didn't do anything wrong. Feeling that around my fingers, the clench of your tight fucking pussy, makes me want to put my cock inside you, but if I fuck you now, I *will* rip you apart." He forces me to take a step back, my thighs hitting the front bumper. "I don't want to hurt you like I've hurt others, so get your sexy fucking ass dressed and get in the car before I rip you in two and make you hate me."

Chapter Eleven

Lex

Selena stays silent beside me. I'm not sure if it's because I scared her when I showed her how much control it took to hold myself back in the woods or if she's starting to realize the gravity of where we're going the closer we get to her home. She became culpable once she gave me the directions to her house.

"What's the matter, rabbit?" I ask.

"Nothing," she whispers. But I know she's lying.

I smirk at her. "Are you mad I didn't fuck you back there? Or are you worried about what I'll do to you once I get you home?" I reach over and brush her hair from her face. "Or are you scared of what I'll do to your husband?"

She draws her face from my touch.

I drop my hand to her inner thigh, pull her legs apart, and grip the skin where her bruises are. "He sealed his fate when he put those on you and I saw them. Piece of shit like that doesn't deserve you."

I hate it but it's true. She's the first woman I've felt

something for. I'm not sure what I'm feeling because I've never felt it before, but it's *something*. When I saw those bruises, I felt like I needed to protect her and get vengeance for her pain. Why else would I risk getting caught again for some pussy?

She isn't just that, though. Her pussy may be incredible, but there's so much more there. Even though we're from totally different worlds, I recognize some of her pain. I see someone who's been let down by every single person in their life, just like me. Where we differ is that she swallows it, letting it eat her away from the inside instead of becoming angry and violent. I sacrificed my freedom to make people feel some of the pain I felt.

I'm trying so hard to give her the freedom she deserves.

"Answer me," I say as I rub her thigh where I'd grabbed. "What's bothering you?"

She looks up at me, her lips drawn tight. "I feel bad for being excited."

I smile at her. "Oh, bunny, I'm rubbing off on you." My hand continues up her thigh. "But don't let too much of me inside you. You're too good for him, but also way too fucking good for me."

The way she pouts her lips at my words makes me want to pull over and rip through her in the most selfish way possible, as if she was the last woman I'd be inside before I go back to prison.

Which she probably is.

"Why didn't you sleep with me back there?" she asks. Finally.

I love that she asked me that. Fucking love it. It means she wants it. She wants me however I need to give it to her. "Remember when you said you didn't really trust me? I don't trust myself, either. I was going to hurt you back there in the woods. Not intentionally, of course, but I was just a wiggle of your hips away from being beyond the point of control."

I expect her to flinch or become scared of me, but her expression remains soft and a little curious. It slightly angers me as images of my past flash through the front of my mind. She doesn't realize what she's flirting with or what losing control really means. She's so naïve to the dangers of a man like me who has nothing to lose and absolutely everything to gain. She doesn't realize I could have shoved her face into the car's hot metal and fucked her until she begged me to stop. Her pleas would only make me savor every thrust. She doesn't grasp how little I cared about having to kill her in the beginning, or that even though I care now, I would still kill her if I had to.

She may have gotten the dirty and feral dog to lick her hand, but I'm not the sweet little pet she wants me to be. I'll still maul her, no matter how much I appreciate her kindness.

"I need you so fucking bad, bunny. I want to pull over on one of these rural roads and bring you into the backseat and—" My breath catches in my throat, silencing my voice. A cop car drives by, and the officer stares at me. I don't breathe again until I'm sure he won't turn around.

"Bad idea, huh?" she asks, though it's clear.

"In the daytime? Yeah. Seems so." I groan and rub the front of my pants.

She reaches out and replaces my hand with her own. She rubs up my length, the denim causing such pleasurable friction beneath her hand. I grab her wrist and stop her. "Not now, bunny. I want to feel this frustration for a while longer. I don't want to come in your hand. I want to be inside you."

It's odd because I almost enjoy the frustrated twitch of my cock. It's something I haven't felt in a while. I didn't wait to get my pleasure when I felt it in the past. I got instant gratification, one way or another.

The ache of staying off her almost feels . . . good. The control feels foreign.

I know I'll get to her eventually, and it will feel amazing when I spill all of myself inside her.

She looks at me with a similar longing, and I wish I could give her what she wants, but it'll have to wait.

She gestures to an exit, and I take the turn that brings us closer to her home. I pull into a fast-food parking lot just off the exit. She looks at the building with a mouth-watering stare. We've been getting quick and easy things to eat, mostly from gas stations, since the beginning. I always thought the less we were seen, the better, but I know she's hungry for a real meal when I hear her stomach growl beside me.

I park the car but instead of getting out, I lean over, grab her face, and pull her into me for a kiss. Her lips spread on mine with a similar hunger. She grabs my hair with one of her hands, as if she's remembering how it felt to pull me into her pussy with a similar grasp. I growl at her touch, struggling to control myself as I remember how she felt when she came around my fingers.

I pull away from her. I have to before I lose myself—or rather, find myself.

"Goddamn it, bunny," I whisper before giving her a final kiss, her lower lip between my teeth as I ease away. "You just wait until I can get my hands on your pussy again." My hand drifts up her thigh and I palm her, making her tremble. She's so warm and wet. Even through her leggings, I can feel it. It's addictive, and I don't ever want to pull my hand away from her. She melts into my touch, and I hope she's only thinking of how I make her feel.

I glance around the parking lot. No one is paying attention to us. I won't fuck her or let either of us expose ourselves, but she's so in need of her orgasm, and I don't want to deny her.

I move my seat back and help her onto my lap. She straddles my waist the best she can, and I pull her mouth to mine. "Grind on my dick, sweet bunny. Make yourself come."

She bites her lower lip before kissing me.

She. Kisses. Me.

She rocks her hips on my lap, and I feel her warmth through not only her pants but my own. I groan as she moves over my hardened length. It's immature, like two teenagers not ready for sex, but it feels so goddamn good. I'm not sure if it's because I'm already so frustrated, but she rubs back and forth, and it hits the head of my dick every fucking time. I wrap my arms around her waist, pulling her closer and trying to keep her from hitting the head so I don't bust. I'm much too old to come in my jeans.

She feels so good in my arms, like she's exactly where she should be. The world grows hazy until all I can see is her and the motions of her hips and chest as she chases her orgasm.

Her moans. Those goddamn moans as she gets herself closer drive me crazy. Her body tenses and the motions of her hips grow ragged.

"Come for me, bunny."

She grips my hair and grinds on me, panting in my ear. She leans into me and moves her hips in a shallow motion as she pushes herself over her edge. Aside from a subtle twitch of her pussy as she rides out her orgasm, she keeps still. Her moans and the warm throb of her on my lap almost make me come, too.

I kiss her and reach between us to feel the wet spot that soaked through her pants and into the front of my jeans. "You made such a mess," I say against her mouth. "Such a good girl. So fucking wet."

I reach down the front of her pants, feeling just how much she came. She looks down at me with the sweetest and most satiated expression I've ever seen.

She looks . . . happy.

I pull my hand from her pants and lick my fingers. She tastes incredible. She always tastes better after she comes for me. I run my wet fingers up the curve of her neck and lace both of my hands behind it. I bring her forehead to mine and hold her there. I never thought I'd be so attracted to a woman like her. She's spoiled but not spoiled rotten. There's still so much good inside her, a brokenness that keeps her from becoming what I hate. She's become something I want with every fiber of my being.

It will be so hard to leave her once I kill her husband, but living on the lam isn't for someone like her. As much as I don't *want* to leave her behind, at least I can leave the states knowing she's safe at home. She can find someone who makes her feel like I do without being me, the dog she can't trust because he can't trust himself.

Chapter Twelve

Selena

I don't realize how hungry I am until I scarf down my food. It's the first substantial meal I've had since the night Lex got in my car. My last big dinner was left-over food-truck pizza on the overtime shift from hell.

"I probably should have fed you sooner," he says through a laugh.

My cheeks heat as I realize I probably looked like a ravenous animal. I pretty much am.

"Worst captor ever," I say through a noisy sip of my nearly empty drink.

Lex smirks at me. "I'm not a captor. You're just an unwilling passenger. We're close, aren't we?" he asks, and I nod. "Then you drive. Drop me off a few blocks away and tell me the address."

I shake my head. I do *not* like that plan. I'm terrified to walk into the house alone after all this. After everything we've done and the things we'll do in the future. "What am I even supposed to tell him about where I've been?"

"Just tell him the truth. That you were carjacked."

"I don't want to go in alone," I whisper.

"You have to. Have I ever let anything bad happen to you?" he asks.

I cock my head at him because he almost sold me, and I'd say that was something pretty fucking bad. "You offered me as payment for that fake ID."

"I didn't let it happen, rabbit," he says. He gets out of the car, and we swap seats.

I tighten my lips as I sit in the driver's seat. I don't like this idea. I hate it, actually. But he's right. I can't pull into my driveway with Lex in the passenger seat. He needs the element of surprise once I get inside the house.

We creep closer to my home without speaking. My stomach twists in knots, more so than when I first had sex with Lex. I pull over before we get into the upscale neighborhood I used to call home. It doesn't feel like it any longer. It feels like a stranger's street. It *is* a stranger's street.

I'm not the same Selena who last drove on this road.

I cut the engine, but we don't move a muscle. "Give me your house key," he says. He reaches toward me with an outstretched hand, but I hesitate before leaning over and twisting the key from the ring.

I hand it to him and cut my gaze.

He gets out of the car and leans through the open door to look at me once more. His hand digs around in his pocket before revealing a pocketknife. He tosses it on the passenger seat. "I'll be there for you as soon as I can. If anything happens, use that, okay?" His hand grips the door handle. It's as if he doesn't want to leave me, or like he has something more he wants to say.

But he doesn't.

I watch him walk away as I turn the key in the ignition and drive toward my hell. The devil is waiting for me, and I want to vomit from the fear squeezing my stomach.

Will he smell Lex on me? Inside me? Will he know I've become a willing participant? I had so many opportunities to escape, but I didn't. Escape meant running back to the nightmare my husband and I share.

I pull into my driveway and stare at the house that doesn't feel like my home anymore. I feel safer in my car. Safer with Lex. I tuck the pocketknife into my waistband and exit the car. The moment I step onto the first stair, the door whips open. A fog drifts over me as I stare at Bryce. He looks so cold, and his hardened mask shows no emotion, not even concern or excitement at seeing me. This blank nothingness is scarier than his rage.

His face finally twists into a familiar anger—the expression I'm used to. I see it in a renewed light this time, as if there's a bullseye planted in the middle of his forehead now, and it almost makes me laugh. I *enjoy* the idea that this might be his last anger-fueled inhale.

Bryce grabs my arm and rips me inside. The sharp points of his fingers dig into my flesh, painting another bruise on my skin.

"Where the hell have you been, Selena?"

I strain against his grasp. "I got carjacked," I say through gritted teeth.

"Bullshit. Stop fucking lying to me."

My eyes well with tears. "I'm not lying to you. I swear."

I'm not lying, but I'm not telling the truth, either. Yes, I got carjacked, but then this whole road trip became something else entirely, something that made me see life in a different way, and I welcomed Lex into my home to get rid of my problems.

"It's been days. Who did you run off with? Have you been fucking around on me?"

"I didn't run off!" I take a deep breath, trying to push away the stampede of guilt that seeks to trample my voice. "I haven't done anything."

"Fucking whore," he says with a curl of his lip.

"Bryce, please . . ." I plead. Such a familiar sound, yet it never made him stop. Pleading only angers him. He hates the weakness.

He silently broods, which is worse than when he yells. His fist pulls back, and before I can react, he punches me in the face. The force knocks me into the wall, and framed pictures fall and shatter at my feet. *Hurry Lex,* I think as the glass spreads along the floor. I don't make a sound, though, because I know he gets off on it. I can't even reach up and baby the stinging heat in my cheek.

He's never hit me in the face like this because it would be too hard to hide. His attacks have always targeted places my clothes could conceal. Everyone probably thought I ran off, and he has no reason to tell them I returned. He can kill me and no one will know any different, and that's what I'm afraid of.

"You want to run off and be a whore? I'll show you how whores get fucked." Bryce grabs me by my hair, leads me to the kitchen, and bends me over the island. A mug falls off the countertop and crashes to the ground as I fight against him. I know what's coming.

It's not the first time.

I slip my hand down and grab the pocketknife from my waistband, concealing it in my balled fist. Cold air bites my skin as he pulls down my pants and works open his fly.

"You don't even have underwear on? My god, Selena. I'm embarrassed to call you my wife." The heat of his cock presses against me, and I pray he doesn't notice the wetness that came from someone other than my husband.

From Lex.

I clench my eyes closed and try to ignore Bryce's harsh grasp as he readies himself. I slip into my mind, where Lex still lives. I try to imagine him behind me. Tears slip past my closed eyes and drip onto the marble countertop. My pelvis rubs painfully against the lip of the island as he pushes his weight against me. I feel guilt, a lot of it, but not for allowing Lex to be inside me. I feel guilty for not fighting harder against Bryce. There's a certain level of acceptance that lets shitty husbands do more than they should to their wives.

Clapping.

The sound forces my eyes to open. Lex stands a few feet away, smacking his hands together in sarcastic applause. Bryce stops and tucks himself back in his pants before zipping them. Only a moment later and he'd have made Lex a liar when he said no one else would get inside me.

Lex draws his pistol and aims it at him. "Don't stop on my account." He circles us, stops across from me, and leans against the island. His eyes meet mine for a moment before returning to Bryce. "She feels fucking amazing, doesn't she?"

"Who the fuck are you?" Spit flies against the back of my arm from the raging force of Bryce's words.

"The one who held your wife against her will," Lex says with a proud, dark smile.

"I told you I wasn't lying," I whisper, though I doubt he hears me over the anger between his ears.

"Is that how you'd fuck her, boss?" Lex asks Bryce. "Come on, show me."

My gaze rises to Lex, but he avoids my eyes as he looks over my head. I drop my forehead to the counter. The shame makes me wish for death all over again. Anger greets me in every direction, and I'm stuck in the middle of a sea of hatred.

"You're pitiful. You can stop or you can fuck her, but mark my words, it'll be the last time you're inside her," Lex says with a disgustingly calm demeanor. I don't know how he's so willing to let Bryce have sex with me, after—

Bryce pulls away from me, and I nearly lose my balance. I go to tug up my pants, but Lex clears his throat.

"Oh no, not yet." The darkness in his eyes makes me tremble. I hardly recognize him. He doesn't look like the man I've let inside me. He looks evil. He's someone else entirely at this moment.

Lex walks up to Bryce and throws him against the wall, and a nauseating *crack* blows through the kitchen when his fist collides with Bryce's face. Blood splatters on the floor, but I can't bring myself to look at the source of it.

With his gun aimed at Bryce, Lex circles behind me and rubs a firm hand down my back. "I thought I'd like watching you fuck her because I've thought about it as I've made her come from my hand, but that was fucking pitiful."

Bryce charges at Lex, but a quick jut of his gun keeps Bryce back.

"If you take another step toward me, I'll blow your brains onto the picture behind you. The one of you and her." Lex goes to unbutton his jeans. Before he goes for the zipper, he turns to Bryce once more. "This stain on my pants? I'm glad you asked. Yeah, it's her come. How often have you worn her like that? Have you even made her come since you fucking married her or is that"—he gestures between me and Bryce—"what she used to get? Some half-assed fuck. I mean, I'm selfish as *fuck* and I still made sure she came."

Lex loops his arm around my hip and puts his hand between my legs. I steal a quick glance at Bryce. His nostrils flare with rage. His face is painted the color of the blood dripping from his nose.

Lex rubs my clit in a way that makes me twitch. "Do you even know how your wife likes to be touched? What makes her do . . . that?" He draws circles around me with the tips of his fingers. "Do you know how many fingers she likes inside her? How about how she likes a tongue on her? God, have you ever tasted her?" He pulls his fingers away from me and licks them. "She's fucking delicious."

"You have no idea who you're fucking with," Bryce snarls.

Lex smirks. "Oh, I do. Someone who doesn't give a shit about his wife. You're a little bitch who beats her even though she's the most—" He swallows hard, as if he has more to say but thinks better of it.

I let the tears fall without restraint. When he takes a step back, I collapse to the floor and press my back against the island. Lex holds an open palm toward me, but he isn't offering me a hand. He wants the knife. He doesn't want to shoot him in this neighborhood—the cops would be called the moment the sound punctuated the serene setting—but I keep the knife pinned to my chest. It makes me feel safer. He looks around for another weapon since my trembling hand refuses to relinquish the pocketknife.

Bryce sees an opportunity and leaps at him. He reaches for the knife attached to a magnet above the island. Lex tucks the pistol behind him before their bodies clash. The sound of flesh on flesh is nauseating. I shut my eyes to hide the view and cover my ears to stop the sound. Blood splashes across me, hitting my face and arms. I'm afraid to look and see who it came from, whose life force has spread across my skin.

I open my eyes.

Bryce stumbles back. Blood runs down his shirt and pants and collects at his feet. He clutches his abdomen, and I scream.

It happened.

It's so fucking real.

Oh god.

Lex clamps a bloody hand over my mouth and tosses the kitchen knife aside. "Shh, bunny," he whispers in that sweet way I recognize as so different from the way he talked before.

"Selena," Bryce whispers. He hits the wall and slides down. "Come here," he says, in a way that is so unlike him.

Lex becomes familiar to me at the same moment Bryce becomes a stranger. It's a desperation I've never seen. It draws me to him. It's a force I can't fight, even if I try. I crawl toward him, shaking off Lex's hand as he tries to grab me. I kneel in front of him, my eyes wide with fear and something else. Something unexpected.

He's dying, I feel it. It nauseates me. It fucking hurts. But . . . it's not pain from the prospect of losing him. It's because the thought of his death doesn't elicit *enough* pain.

I swipe open the blade and stab it into his stomach. All the evilness inside him spills from the wound. I pull it out and stab it through his groin. Lex gasps behind me, and there's a squelching sound as I snatch the knife out and stab him again and again.

"*Fuck you, you fucking asshole!*" I keep stabbing until strong arms wrap around me and pull me away. My arm continues its repeated downward arc toward Bryce, fighting against Lex's grasp as my rage blinds me.

Lex gets control over me, and his hand rides down my arm and grabs the knife. He rubs the handle on his shirt and puts it in his pocket.

"Rabbit, we have to go." He grabs my wrist.

I shake my head. "Fuck me first." I can feel the evil behind my glare when I turn my darkened eyes to him. The need to hurt Bryce one last time. I expect him to fight me on it, but he wastes no time pulling me into him.

His warm breath races across my chilled skin. "You're out of your mind, rabbit. You weren't supposed to get involved. You weren't supposed to touch him." He grabs my bloodied hand and rubs it. "You aren't a killer. You can't be," he whispers. "That's not what was supposed to happen."

"I want this, Lex," I say with more surety than I've ever felt about anything in my life.

He looks at me. "You know I'd do anything for you. If you want me to fuck you, I'll fuck you." Lex turns me around and puts my hands on the counter again. He unzips his pants and pulls out his cock. He pulls down my pants and pushes himself inside me.

I gasp as I drop my head to the marble, and the world disappears again, dripping away like the blood on the floor. He fucks me, hard and selfish, tearing me apart in ways I've never felt. It doesn't matter how wet I am for him; he still makes me ache with the force of his thrusts.

Knowing Bryce is watching, he fucks me differently, and I don't expect anything less. Lex loves control, and nothing screams it more than fucking someone's wife in front of them. He bottoms out inside me and pushes just a fraction further, making me whimper.

"Did he ever fuck you like this?" Lex growls in my ear as he grinds his hips against my ass. "He looked like a disappointing fuck."

"No, he never fucked me like you do," I pant, leaving the fog of my breath on the fancy countertop. Lex groans and runs his arms down mine, leaning his weight into me.

Bryce chokes out a gurgled whimper—a sign of life, albeit a weak one. Lex goes to pull out of me to take care of it, but I grab his shirt. "Don't. I hope he feels it all. I hope he can see us."

"Sadistic fucking rabbit," Lex growls as he pushes himself deep again. "I'm not ready to come yet. Not here." He looks around, eyeing the steps. "Take me to your room."

He pulls out of me and turns me to face him. His hand wipes the blood on my face.

"I want to fuck you in his bed. Your bed," he says, low and smooth, as if we didn't just kill a man.

I bite my lip and tug up my pants as he zips his jeans. With one last glance at Bryce's motionless body, I guide Lex up the stairs. Desire saturates each warm exhale as it leaves his lips and sends pebbles across my skin. The wetness between my legs soaks through my pants.

When my hand grips the doorknob to our bedroom, it feels foreign, like I never belonged here at all. The door drags on the light blue carpet as it opens. It's only through new eyes, gray-colored glasses, that I see how little of myself is in this room. Bryce's suits line the closet, and his drab ties hang on the outside of the closet door. The room is decorated to his liking—black, white, and dark shades of gray. Nothing screams that a wife slept in here except my perfume—his favorite—on the nightstand. My clothes folded in the drawers, away and out of sight, as he commanded.

Lex walks past me and rubs his blood-soaked hand across the white comforter. A sadistic smile crosses his face as he smears more crimson across the blanket, as if he's painting on a canvas. He lies back with a groan and motions me to him. "Come on, bunny," he whispers. "Get on my lap. I haven't gotten to see you ride my dick outside of a damn car."

I remove my pants and climb over him, straddling his lap as he undoes his zipper again. His warm cock rests against his lower stomach. His hand runs down the front of my thighs, where the worst of my fading bruise remains. The touch unintentionally fills my mind with memories, and I flinch.

"It's over," he says as he brings my face to his to kiss me. "He'll never hurt you again."

"Lex," I whimper.

He wraps his hand around his cock with one hand, lifts my hip with the other, and pushes himself inside me. I lower myself onto his lap, welcoming every inch of him

He's right. I haven't had a chance to look at him quite like this. Looking down, I see a man who looks content to just be within me.

His blue eyes meet mine, dark and hungry. I try to ignore the blood soaking his shirt and saturating mine. My husband's blood. When I lift the shirt and expose his abdomen, I see a long gash. It isn't just Bryce's blood after all.

"Lex!" I put my hand to his wound, blood dripping around my fingers.

He bats me away and smirks. "Let me bleed, rabbit. I'm fine. Just focus on riding my cock."

How is he okay? Doesn't he feel it? I'm not fine, and I'm just looking at his injury, not living with it.

He pulls me closer until my chest rests on his. The warm blood soaks through more of my shirt as he grabs my hips and forces me to move. He shows no reaction to the pain as I move with him. In fact, he looks like he almost enjoys it.

He groans, raising his hips to meet mine. "You look fucking beautiful."

I can't remember the last time Bryce called me anything nice, especially not beautiful. I place my hands on either side of his head and kiss his forehead. I leave my lips there, just feeling his warm breath on my throat.

"I'm going to guess he compliments you about as good as he fucks you," Lex says with a laugh.

"Pretty much." I draw my lips tight, keeping them against his forehead.

Lex lifts his hip and flips me onto my back. I stretch out on the king-sized bed, tie-dyed with blood. I wrap my legs around him, and he leans over and kisses me.

"Bunny, you are the sexiest thing I've ever laid my hands on. Fucking. Perfect. So goddamn smart, too. You deserve so much more than that piece of shit. More than me . . ." His words waver at the end until they cut off completely. His expression grows cold and more focused as he drives me into the mattress. Blood drips from his wet shirt onto mine. "I'm going to come, rabbit," he says in a tone I almost don't recognize. It's robotic and distant. His thrusts slow and he pulls out of me, a string of his come connecting me to him.

Lex goes into the bathroom, leaving me half naked and confused. He comes out with a towel pressed on his cut.

"Are you sure you're okay?" I ask.

"Yeah, it's hardly anything. It'll stop," he says. He uses one hand to zip up his pants. "We have to get going. I'll take care of the cleanup here and your car. Wipe out as much of us as I can."

I lean over and pull a key from the nightstand, tossing it

to him. "My old car is in the garage. No one knows about it. Or at least no one who would report him missing right away."

Lex smiles at me, pinched with something I can't recognize.

"I'll grab money, too."

He tosses me a quick nod before heading down the slick wooden staircase.

I pack up some money in a bag. The steps creak beneath my weight as I come back downstairs. I look back once more, inhaling the noxious, metallic scent of blood. With Bryce's spirit heading to hell where it belongs, nothing tethers me to this damn house any longer.

The house that never felt like home.

Chapter Thirteen

Lex

The garage door buzzes and begins to rise. I start to back out, but the door to the house opens. There's no way to avoid her gaze, and she looks more betrayed by the second. I was undecided about leaving her behind until the moment I realized she deserved more than me, so much more than I could ever give her. I knew what I had to do. I *had* to leave her, but I wasn't fast enough. I don't care about the cash or the bloodbath I left behind, but I don't want to see her face. I can't meet her feelings of betrayal.

She's spent too long being betrayed, and I'm doing it to her again.

Selena deserves what Bryce had to offer her, minus him. Now that he's gone, she can go back to normal, a feeling I can never give her.

I hate that I came inside her and left. She deserves so much more than that, but I knew my resolve would weaken if I tried to say goodbye. Now it's too late, and the look of betrayal is even worse than I feared. It makes me feel things that I didn't expect to feel.

She rushes down the steps. Her arms and face are scrubbed, but blood remains on her shirt. She has a change of clothes under one arm and a bag under the other. Her eyes narrow when she tries the door handle and finds it locked. I should have driven away. Put the pedal to the floor and left her. She places her hand against the window, and the broken desperation in her eyes forces me to lower it.

"You were leaving without me?" she asks.

"You can't go, Selena. I can't let you," I tell her, as firmly as I can. I don't want to, but I have to. I can't bring her with me. "Tell the police he assaulted you. Self-defense. You have the bruises. Nothing will happen to you." I've promised her safety, and she'll be safer away from me.

"Really, Lex?" She raises her voice. The garage door is open to the idyllic neighborhood, and she'll draw attention if she keeps this up.

"Lower your fucking voice, rabbit," I snap.

Her lip trembles. "Fuck you! After everything we did! Everything we've been th—"

"For fuck's sake." I unlock the doors. She can't keep yelling like this. "Get in the fucking car."

She stares at me for a moment before dropping into the passenger seat of the SUV. She crouches on the floorboard as we drive away from her old life and into my new one. The new life I don't want to make her a part of, but I have no choice now.

"Get off the fucking floor," I say as I pull her up by her arm. She flinches. "Did he hurt you?" Only once she sits up and allows the sun to touch her skin do I see the bruises forming on her arm and cheek. I fight the urge to reach out and touch them.

I promised her I wouldn't let anything bad happen to her, and she ended up getting beat on and nearly fucked again by that piece of shit. It breaks something inside me. I hear the shattering sound in my chest.

"Bunny," I whisper, "I'd have been there sooner, but your neighbor was putting groceries away and I had to wait for her to close her garage door."

"It's fine."

I shake my head. "It's not."

"I'm more upset that you tried to leave me," she says as she tugs off her shirt, exposing incredible tits that I can't help but stare at as I try to drive.

She puts on a clean shirt and hands me something of Bryce's to wear. I shake my head, but she keeps it held toward me. I grab it and have her hold the wheel as I change. It's too small for me, and my muscles stretch the t-shirt, but it'll work for now.

"You wouldn't understand, Selena, and I'm not getting into it with you. I needed you to listen to me."

"I want to go with you," she whispers.

I raise my voice. "You think I didn't want to take you with me? It's not safe. It's not something we can do together. You weren't supposed to do anything but play the grieving fucking widow." I swallow hard. "And go be fucking happy."

"I want to be with you," she says, a defiant pull in her voice.

I steer to the side of the road and throw the car in park. I turn her face to mine. "I have never felt anything for anyone like I feel for you, and that's why you can't be with me. You need to be free and happy. It took everything in me to let you go. Being with me means prison for you, do you understand that? I carjacked you. I got your address off your ID. I took you back to your house to rob you, and I ended up killing your husband. My fingerprints are everywhere in the car and your house. They were on the kitchen knife." I sigh. "If you don't want to be a victim of domestic violence, be a victim of a botched robbery. I don't care which, just be a goddamn victim, rabbit, please."

As much as it breaks me, she needs to go. Being with me means she's a willing participant in all of it. She'll be as culpable as me. A girl like her wouldn't survive in prison, and we both know that.

If she refuses to be a victim, I'll have to kill her. I'll have no fucking choice.

I wait for her answer, knowing if I'm backed into a corner, I'll give her a humane death before I let her go into the system.

Her eyes narrow. "I stabbed him too."

"I know you fucking did," I say as I brush a hand through my hair.

"We need to get going if we want to make it to the border before he's found." She sits back with a stubborn huff and crosses her arms over her chest. "I don't want to be a victim anymore, Lex." She speaks with such finality, so I don't say another word. I can understand that. At least she has *someone* to look out for her.

Even if that someone is me.

"Toss your shirt out the window," I tell her, and she does. She seems so distant as she sits back and stares out the window. Maybe she realizes the gravity of what we've done. Together. What I tried to save her from.

We drive south, and I almost expect her to tell me to turn around and bring her back home. But that isn't an option any longer. I've stayed long enough in the state I needed to leave the most. The state I left and then returned to.

For her.

I toss out my bloody shirt once we reach the northern tip of Pennsylvania, spreading our evidence across state lines. A stifling silence hangs between us. I don't know what to say to her, and she sure as hell doesn't know what to say to me. I look over, and she's staring at me.

"What's on your mind, rabbit?" I ask. I look at the rearview mirror, pull the rabbit's foot from my pocket, and hang it up. Whether it's lucky or not, it's become an icon of our fucked-up little relationship.

Her eyes narrow. "What happened back there."

"Elaborate." I'm getting annoyed with her evasiveness when I know she wants to talk about it.

"You acted weird." She swallows. "Like you wanted him to have sex with me."

I shake my head. I didn't intend for it to happen, I truly didn't, but when I saw it happening, the sick part of me wanted him to keep going. I watched them at first because I thought I wanted it. I had thought about it enough times to at least learn how it made me feel when I actually saw it, but when I realized how much it broke her, I decided to break him instead.

"I thought I wanted to watch. It's something I've fantasized about," I say.

She chews the inside of her cheeks and drops her gaze.

"Turns out, I didn't. I couldn't."

Her gaze shoots to me. "Why were you saying those things about him, then?"

I knew calling out her husband for being a pitiful lover would hurt his pride and crush him before I could even touch him. When he found out I knew how to touch his wife, how to make her feel good and make her come, I knew it would break him. Showing him the come stain on my jeans forced him to realize she'd been a willing participant. It was physical proof of our affair. I went too far with it, though. I disappeared into the shadow of who I was before I met Selena. I hid from the light she cast on me as she tried to draw me from the darkness. But then she stabbed him, dragging herself into the darkness with me. The moment she pushed that knife through him, I knew I'd caused that. I pushed her to be the woman who was on her knees, stabbing the man who hurt her. I transformed her into me, but I don't want her to be me.

I wanted more for her, and that's when I knew I had feelings for her. That's why I tried to leave her. I don't want her to be a predator. I need her to be Selena, the sweet little rabbit that slept with a wolf.

I grip the steering wheel. "You seem to selectively forget what I am. I'm a killer. I didn't intend to just kill your husband. I wanted him to hurt, really fucking hurt, before I killed him."

"I just don't understand why you would tell him to keep going," she whispers.

"Because that wasn't me in there. That's the person I was before you. I was thinking about inflicting pain instead of thinking about you." I pull to the side of the road again and reach for her, ignoring her flinch of mistrust. I draw her into me. "He needed to know it would be the last time he'd be inside you. It was all mental warfare, and I'm sorry you were collateral damage in that war." I press my forehead against hers. It's such a battle inside me sometimes, and I have no way of explaining that to her. Not really. "The moment I realized how pissed off it made me, there's no way I could let him fuck you, rabbit. Trust me on that."

"Why'd you stop fucking me in the kitchen? Was it because of him?"

"God no." I smirk at the thought of the moment she surpassed me in a way I never expected. She wanted me to fuck her in front of her dying husband. That turned me on more than ever before. Her vengeance was delicious, and I was happy to be a part of it. I gave her what she wanted, but I didn't want it to end there. My balls ached to unload in her, and she felt incredible, but I wanted to fuck her in their marital bed. Even when I was ready to bust, I realized she was better off without me and that I had to push her away. I shouldn't have let myself come then, but I couldn't help it. That sick part of me wanted to leave her dripping with my come.

When I lean into her, I smell the soap she used to clean herself, a variation of the same flowery soap I used to wash away the blood. She'd have gotten rid of all traces of me before she changed her pants. I don't care that she cleaned herself and changed her clothes, but she better not have any panties on. She knows how I feel about them.

When my hand slips down the front of her pants, she whimpers out a moan. There's nothing between my hand and her pussy. *Good girl.* I growl before kissing her. I have plans for her. She's along for the ride now, whether I like it or not, and I intend to claim her as my own—*truly* my own— until death parts us.

"Wait until it gets dark, bunny, because that pussy is mine."

TOWERING maple trees surround both sides of us, as if the road has cut the woods in half. I pull the car onto the shoulder and park as deep as I can in the brush, trying to conceal the vehicle. Branches scrape the paint until we're in our own little alcove of seclusion.

"Get in the backseat," I say. She wastes no time climbing over the center console and melting into the bench seat's buttery leather. There's no way I'm climbing over shit, so I get out and open the back door.

The overhead light illuminates her, and her eyes are big and tempting. I climb into the roomy backseat, and the light flickers off when I close the door. Darkness surrounds us with a heavy blackness that reminds me of the first night I slept with her in the back of her other car.

"Last chance to back out," I whisper as I lean over her. I can't see more than her silhouette, but I bask in the heat of her beneath me. I'm giving her one more chance to change her mind before I make her pussy mine for good.

"I'm not backing out," she says.

I undo my pants and lower the zipper. I run my hand along her neck and chest by mere memory. When I go to remove her pants, she lifts her hips to help me. I rest my cock against her pussy. She feels so warm and welcoming as she throbs beneath me. I lean down and kiss her.

She's so wet. All it takes is pulling my hips back enough to push inside her. I groan as I go deep from the very first thrust, hitting the end of her. A melodic whimper breaks through the stagnant air.

"God, bunny, you have me by the balls, you know that?" I whisper before nipping her throat.

I'm destined for hell but her pussy is heaven, and I'll be saved as long as I'm inside her. I'm washed of my sins as long as I bathe in her come.

Selena moans as I angle myself just right, rubbing her in all the ways I've learned she likes. I know what makes her moan and sends her body into waves of trembling pleasure. Her nails rake my back and her hips move beneath me, getting me too close too soon. The more I try to prolong it, lengthening and slowing my thrusts, the more her pussy squeezes me for more. I don't know why I feel the need to come, and I sure as hell don't want to do it so soon, but she creates a feeling of euphoria inside me.

She's going to stay by my side—she's *choosing* to stay by my side—and my mind is a hundred percent focused on her right now. I start to imagine an "us." We became a team, after all, a pairing in blood that neither of us can wash away.

"I'm going to come," I tell her. I can't see it, but I know her face is painted with disappointment. As her hips buck into mine, I know she wants more. Shit, I want more, too, but my balls tighten and I'm going to come whether we want it or not. I kiss her as my thrusts slow, and the growl that comes from my throat vibrates the air. It feels so good to spill myself inside her. I don't want it to end, and I won't let it.

I sit back, my cock spent but still hard. "Come here, sweet bunny. I'm not done with you."

Her silhouette crosses the backseat, and she straddles my lap with her bare thighs. I push myself back inside her, past the warm stickiness of my come. I wrap my arms around her and draw her into me. She nestles against my chest.

I begin to soften, losing my erection as I overstay my welcome inside her. I don't care, though. It still feels so good to be within her tight, warm pussy. A warm drop of my come slips from inside her, running down my dick and landing on my pelvis. She leans back, and I take the opportunity to rub her clit. She twitches with pleasure, making the walls of her pussy clench around me.

"I'm going to stay inside you for as long as I can," I tell her as I brush hair from her face. "Until I can fuck you again."

I rub her clit with a side-to-side motion of my thumb, thrumming the hood until she trembles on my lap. Every twitch of her pussy draws blood straight to my dick. She awakens me with the warm heat of her body on my lap.

Selena drops her head to the crook of my neck, her chest rising heavily against mine as I work her toward the edge. The closer she gets to coming, the more she breathes life into my dick. Her incredible moans carry the blood through my veins and toward my cock.

"Come, sweet bunny. Come on my dick and make me hard again so I can fuck you through your orgasm," I growl as she rides my lap, grinding against my fingers.

She moans my name in the throes of her orgasm. It's worth all that I've done to hear that because it led me right to this moment, with Selena coming on my dick.

As her body tenses and tightens, the spasms awaken me until I'm hard again, filling her as I grow. I meet her with a thrust of my hips, and she screams out from the pleasure of riding out her orgasm with my cock stretching her once more.

"Good fucking girl," I growl as I hold her hips and thrust harder. The wet sounds of our mingling come intensifies. It's a sound I'll always remember because it's an audible rendition of how good she makes me feel every time I'm inside her.

My come drips down the length of my dick, smearing across my skin as I thrust into her. I reach between us, swiping two of my fingers through a pool of my come on my pelvis. I see her face, illuminated by the moonlight. Moans roll from her loose lips. I bring my fingers up to them and push my come into her mouth. Her lips close around my fingers, and the look she gives me brings me close to busting all over again.

I grab both sides of her face and kiss her, taking the taste of my come into my mouth. "Do you want me to fill you again?" I ask as I draw away from her.

She whimpers out her answer, her face nodding against my neck as she drops her mouth to my skin.

"Your husband never came inside you, and yet you're on my lap, willing to let me fill you a second time."

She moans against me, her body tensing at the mention of her husband. I lift her to put her on her back once more. I never pull out of her, not for a second. I want to stay buried inside her where I belong.

I reach between us and rub her clit, sticky with my come and her own wetness. Every time I push myself as far as I can inside her, more of the intertwined pleasure slips onto my dick. Her moans are the only other sound I focus on, the growing screams lengthening and becoming hoarse the harder and faster I fuck her. She covers her mouth to keep from crying out, and I lean over and tug her hand away from her face.

"I want to hear those sounds leaving your mouth."

"God, Lex, you're too deep," she whispers, and I realize just how much of my cock I'm making her take. Every fucking inch. I'm deep enough that I feel her still swollen clit against my pelvis.

I draw back, giving her a fraction of relief. "Have you ever been spit on?" I ask.

"What?"

"Has your husband ever spit on your pussy?"

She shakes her head fast enough to make me certain she's never had such a disrespectful thing done to her.

I reach over and push my thumb into her mouth, tugging her lower lip as I pull it out. I lean down and spit on her pussy, the warm wetness dripping down her clit and spreading around my cock. It isn't a disrespectful gesture. Quite the contrary. I respect no one else the way I respect her. She lets out a soft moan that surprises us both.

"Oh, bunny, you liked that?"

Unwilling to face her own shame, she doesn't answer me. I push my thumb back into her mouth and graze her lower lip before raising her chin.

"Open your mouth," I say. My spit on her pussy isn't enough, and I'm sure no one's ever spit in her pretty mouth, either. She hesitates, and I stare at her full lips as I wait for her to do as she's told. "Come on, sweet bunny, open up for me." My voice is low and rich with pleasure.

I hit the overhead light because I want to see it all. She spreads her lips for me, and my cock twitches at the sight. Part of me wants to pull out and put her incredible mouth on my dick, make her taste us both, but I want to be inside her pussy more.

I smirk as I lean over her, my mouth watering with anticipation. Not often do you get to do such an act to a woman so above you. At this moment, it doesn't matter how much more money and power she has. She's below me.

I spit in her mouth. A startled yelp leaves her throat as it hits her tongue. I know she doesn't want to like it, but it's clear her body does as she clenches around me.

"You've taken all I've given you," I groan as I thrust deeper. I'm getting close again, feeling the walls of her pussy tightening around me. The thought of filling her again, giving her another load that claims her as mine, shoves me closer to my edge.

Something about spilling my pleasure into her and keeping her on my dick until I could fuck and fill her again makes me forget about everything around us. It makes me forget about our crimes. I forget that we're running from the law.

I come. A low and gravelly groan vibrates her mouth as I kiss her. I put my hand around the base of my dick as I draw away from her and sit up. When I'm most of the way out, my tip still twitches inside her. A trail of come washes along my dick. There's so much come. She's a fucking mess as I pull out of her. I gather as much as I can with the tips of my fingers and push it back inside her. I graze her clit as I draw my fingers away.

"You look so fucking sexy covered in my come," I growl. She does. She's spread open for me, coated in two loads, and she has my spit on her tongue.

We're from two different worlds, but only a thick layer of our remnants separates us now. We're in a place where pain and suffering can only be cured by pleasure.

A place where there are no rules or laws.

A place where wolves sleep with their prey.

Chapter Fourteen

Selena

I can't believe I let Lex spit on me. I've never had such a degrading thing done to me in my life. But when he was over me, with his lips pouting and his tongue moving to gather his spit, I let him. I'd let him do just about anything to me. Hell, I was even willing to let him kill me. A little spit is nothing in comparison.

The spit didn't bother me as much as the way my body responded to it. The wet warmth made me throb. I watched it fall from his perfect lips and move toward my mouth in slow motion, and my stomach tightened with excitement. I hated that I liked it, but I loved how big and powerful he felt above me as his spit lived on my tongue. I swallowed a piece of him, taking it deep into my stomach while his cock drove upward.

"What's on your mind, rabbit?" Lex asks as I drive. His words rip me from my thoughts. I don't know how to answer him. Everything blurs together and makes it hard for me to focus on any one thing.

Red and blue flashes light up behind us.

"Fuck!" Lex says. He doesn't look scared or panicked. He looks angry—annoyed with me and the situation. I've never seen fear on his face, and I don't think I ever will. He flips down the mirror and brushes his hair over the tattoo along his hairline. He's not panicking, but I am. My breath hitches as I pull to the side of the darkened highway.

Lex reaches over and grabs my chin, forcing me to look at him. "If things go south, put your seat down and get out of my way." He gestures to the pistol tucked into his waistband. "You need to get your shit together, little rabbit. You look like a bunny who's seen movement in the bushes—back straight as an arrow, nose flaring, eyes wide. I need you to be brave, or we're both fucked. Do you understand that?"

"Lex . . ." I whisper with a shake of my head that won't stop. I'm *trying* not to panic, but my nerves are rubbing raw from the inside out. I look so out of place beside Lex, and the guilt I feel from all the murders I've witnessed simmers beneath my skin, ready to ooze from me.

You've lied to the police before, I remind myself, trying to harness the bravery Lex thinks I possess. I seek the confidence that concealed my bruises so many times before.

"You can do it, rabbit," he says as he moves his fingers from my chin to brush the hair off my face, wiping cold sweat from my cheeks. His words make me swell with a strength I didn't have moments before. With his encouragement, I feel like I can do anything.

Including lying to the law.

When I hear the heavy footfalls outside the window, I lower it. The officer leans down to look at me, shining a blinding light in my face. The plastic expression I've used to cover for Bryce paints my face once more. "Good evening, officer," I say, trying to control the tremble in my fingers by gripping the steering wheel.

"Nearly morning, miss," he says as he leans closer to look beyond me. Lex is slumped over, as if he's sleeping.

"Yeah, I guess it is." I smile and gesture to Lex. "I got the crappy shift," I whisper.

The officer tightens his lips. "Do you know why I pulled you over?"

"Not a clue," I tell him, envisioning his sweet features blown off by a bullet if I fuck this up. The thought keeps me calm. I refuse to let this man die tonight because of me.

"You were hitting the lines on the shoulder pretty frequently. Have you had anything to drink tonight?"

I chuckle. "God no. I'm just really tired, and there's not another rest stop for a little ways."

The officer leans in and gets uncomfortably close to my mouth. Satisfied that he doesn't smell any alcohol on my breath, he looks over at Lex. "Can he drive instead?"

"I'm sure he could," I say, but when the officer just keeps staring at me, I prod Lex's arm. "Honey," I whisper, and it feels so weird to call him that. I hope the officer doesn't notice. "Hey?" I say louder, prodding harder.

Lex lifts his head, making a show of a dramatic yawn. "What's going on?" he asks, a believable confused look on his face.

"She was driving a bit reckless. Says she's drowsy. Can you drive the vehicle? I'd prefer to not have it towed."

"Oh, yeah, I can drive. I've been sleeping for . . ." He glances at the clock. "Jesus, like, four hours. Why'd you let me sleep that long, baby?" he asks. Him calling me *baby* feels even weirder than me calling him honey. Of all the things he calls me, baby is *not* one of them.

"Can I have your licenses? Insurance?"

My breath cuts off at my diaphragm, as if it's all sucked out of me with just those few words. I don't know if the insurance is current, and I curse myself for not checking sooner. Bryce didn't want me driving this SUV because it's older, and it wasn't as easy for him to keep tabs on me without all the new gadgets you get in cars these days. I don't know *why* he'd have kept the insurance up to date.

Lex is acutely aware of my panic, and he smiles as he leans forward to pull out the proof of insurance. He puts it in my lap, and I see the end date is current. I hide my relieved breath, exhaling into the empty pockets of my wallet as I rifle through it to find my license. My eyes meet Lex as I reach out and wait for him to produce his fake fucking ID. He remains calm and collected as he pulls it out and hands it over.

The officer cocks his head. "Ben Gurgen Hoffe? That's a unique name."

Lex's calm demeanor breaks as he lets out a small laugh that I see more than I hear. "It's a family name. It's actually pronounced JER-gen." He tightens his lips and sobers. "Here, babe, switch spots. Your turn to nap." He climbs out of the car. Hearing him call me *babe* is even weirder than baby. I hated that he called me rabbit and bunny at first, but now I can't imagine him calling me anything else.

The glint of his pistol winks at me as his shirt rides up, and I can only hope the officer doesn't notice it as well. I undo my seatbelt and open the door, stepping onto the pavement with legs that feel like they'll give out on me. After I sit in the passenger seat, I fasten my seatbelt. I can hardly hear over the whoosh of the blood in my ears. I wipe my sweat-coated palms onto my shirt.

"Krause? Is that of German origin, too?" Lex asks as he leans closer to the officer's nameplate.

The officer looks up at him and smiles. "Yeah, actually. No one notices that."

"Have you visited Germany yet?" Lex leans against the door, looking suave as fuck. Even I forget he's a felon for the moment.

"No, though I always intended to. My remaining grand-parents live near Munich."

Lex shakes his head. "Yeah, you need to go. First off, life's too short, and second, it's a beautiful city. You have to go during Oktoberfest if you want to get the full experience. Maybe don't bring grandma, though." A genuine smile crosses Lex's face, and I almost believe he went to Germany.

The officer laughs. "She'd probably outdrink them all." He taps the IDs against his open palm. "You know what? I don't think we need to make this more than it is. As long as someone who is more awake can drive, I'm fine with it." He glances at me with a scolding look. "Here you go, Mr. Gurgen Hoffe. Please drive safe." He returns Lex's ID.

Lex opens the door to get in the car once the officer steps away.

"Hey," the officer calls back as Lex closes the car door.

Lex leans out the window, his hand moving to his hip and wrapping around the pistol's grip.

"Maybe I'll see you at the next Oktoberfest!" the officer calls out with a final nod of his head.

Lex's shoulders drop and his hand releases from the plastic grip. "If you do, I'll buy you a drink," Lex says with a wave. "Have a good night, officer."

With tight lips, he puts on his seatbelt and drives away from the shoulder. He keeps silent until we're a few miles down the road. "Ben Gurgen Hoffe," Lex says with a shake of his head. I stare at him because I don't get it. "Been

Jerkin' Off." Lex sighs. "Fucking Rodney. If he wasn't already dead, I'd kill him."

I laugh. It rips through me and feels so foreign that it makes my stomach ache. Tears that aren't from pain or fear fall down my cheeks.

"Stop laughing. That was pure fucking luck. I really thought I'd have a dead cop on my hands. On *our* hands."

I can't stop laughing. I rub the rabbit's foot. "Guess it *is* lucky."

Lex's spine slowly relaxes, and his chest falls forward. He finally lets out a small laugh of his own. When he sobers, the tenor of his voice changes. "You need to be more careful when you drive. We're lucky your pea-brained husband kept insurance on this car. I checked before we left." He draws a sharp breath and slowly exhales, a very methodical set of motions he repeats until his rising chest slows. He clears his throat. "You did a great job, bunny," he says with a reassuring rub of my shoulder. "But you have to be careful when you're driving, because luck like that won't happen twice. Even with that damn thing." He gestures toward the rabbit's foot.

Lex brushes back his hair, exposing his tattoo again. "Gurgen Hoffe," Lex says through an annoyed laugh.

"Let it go, Ben," I tell him, a smile drawing my lips upward.

"Aren't you tired? Go to sleep," he commands.

I shake my head. "I'm not tired at all."

"Then why were you driving like shit?"

"Because I had a lot on my mind. I was hugging the fucking shoulder, not the center line. Not a big deal."

"Kind of a big deal, rabbit." He shakes his head this time. "What were you thinking about?"

I scoff. "Nothing."

"Tell me, Selena."

"I was thinking about when you spit on me . . ."

He groans as if he knew that I would bring it up and was waiting for it. "And? What is there to think about?"

I cross my arms over my chest and stare out the window without saying another word. I don't appreciate his attitude about it. He has no idea what direction I was going to go with it, yet he got defensive from the start. Maybe I was going to tell him I fucking liked it, but now, I'm not telling him shit.

"Oh, stop, rabbit. You didn't like it? Did it hurt your little feelings?"

His words and the way he says them enrage me. A fire smolders in my gut. I already felt bad for liking it, but now he's being a condescending fuck about it. I cut my gaze to him and narrow my eyes. "Fuck. You."

"Don't get pissy with me, little girl, or I'll make you sorry for that mouth."

"You won't do anything."

"I'll pull this car over and choke you with my dick until you see stars. I'm serious, Selena. You do *not* want to tempt me."

I throw my hands up. "Why are we even fighting right now?"

"Because you'd rather fight than admit you liked it when I degraded you. That you liked feeling *used* by me."

"I didn't like it," I lie.

His sadistic smirk rubs me all the wrong ways. I hate his annoying smugness. "Whatever helps you sleep at night, rabbit."

We drive in silence. I'm angry enough that I'm thinking about smacking him, but I'm enamored enough that if he angrily told me to suck his dick, I'd drop to my knees without a second thought.

A sign for a lake draws up on our right. Lex looks twice at it. "Well, that will have to do," he whispers, finally breaking the silence. He turns off at the exit and drives toward the lake, following the signs until we reach the blocked entrance to the park. He pulls ahead and takes a dead-end sideroad. The car dips and sways over each pothole. He pulls over, and we get out of the car.

A thin veil of moonlight casts a dim glow over the world around us, leaving us mostly in shadows. Lex walks toward a rusted chain-link fence covered in overgrown brush. He pries at the metal, rattling it before tugging back a broken section. He slips through, and I grab some of the clothes from the car and follow him.

"Hey, wait up," I whisper. The fence claws at my skin as I try to squeeze through. *Thanks for holding it open, asshole.* He doesn't slow down, so I quicken my strides to catch up.

The clearing opens and reveals the lake. I only hear Lex's breathing over the sound of crickets and croaking frogs. A fish surfaces on the other side of the lake, and I hear the ripples it leaves in its wake. It's *that* quiet.

"Get undressed," he says before leaning against a tree and watching me.

I don't want to cave to his demands, especially when I'm still so heated from his attitude, but he has a way of speaking that influences me like nothing ever has. It makes me *want* to do things he asks of me.

I grip the hem of my shirt and begin to lift it.

"Slower," he tells me.

I do as I'm told, removing my shirt as slowly as I can. The heat of his stare is on me, and he watches as I toss my shirt away. The hunger in his expression makes me throb and forget about my annoyance.

I slip my pants down my thighs, and cool air embraces my body. Lex unbuckles his jeans, and I watch as he slips off his pants. My eyes rove down his body. I lock on to the cut on his stomach, glad to see it's stopped bleeding. I still find myself worrying about him, even though he didn't seem to mind being stabbed.

I walk toward the lake and dip my hand into the water to check the temperature. I desperately want to clean up, and it's the best we'll get at this point. Lex brushes past me and gets in, the water spreading around his strong body as he wades deeper.

"Is it cold?" I ask.

"Very. Come on." He motions me in.

I wade into the water, and my breath catches in my throat when it reaches my chest. The blackness stops at the swells of my breasts, nearly covering them. Lex wraps me up in his arms and holds me in front of him. His expression softens for the first time since the interaction in the car.

"It's not the degradation you liked. That isn't who you are."

Lex pushes me under the water and holds me there. I don't flail until my lungs clench for breath, and even then, it's weak. I reach up and grip his wrist, but I don't push him away. I should be scared—that's a normal reaction—but I'm not. I listen to the black emptiness and the thunder of my heart. I almost feel serene, even as my stomach tightens and my lungs scream for air. I just *know* he'll pull me up. I don't know how I know, but I do. I'm safe within his grasp, even in such an unsafe situation.

Even gazing into the cold face of death.

Just as my body begins to lurch for air against my will,

he grabs me beneath my arms and lifts me to the surface. I cough and spit water.

"It's the trust you have in me that makes you wet. Not the act."

I hear the seduction in his voice, though it's muffled by the wet hair sticking to my ears. I spit more water and steady my breathing. "What?" I brush back my hair, hearing the droplets return to the lake and blend with the water.

"When I spit on you. You weren't turned on because you like to be degraded. It's because you trusted me enough to do it to you in the first place. You've let me fuck you, take care of you, shit, even put your life in my hands. It's all trust." He kisses me. "You trust that when I cut off your breath, I'll give it back to you." His mouth finds my clavicle, kissing above my breasts. "You always come because you trust me more than your husband. You trust me more than you trust yourself."

"I-I . . . that's . . ." I try to fight his words, but he's right. I trust him. Everything inside me should mistrust him—he took me at gunpoint, for fuck's sake—but I feel no fear when it comes to him. He holds all of me in his hands, and I never worry he'll drop me.

"You'd let me do anything to you, wouldn't you, bunny?"

I gnaw at the insides of my cheeks and swallow before my eyes rise to meet his. "Yes," I whisper.

"Would you let me fuck your ass?" he asks, so casually.

My mouth drops open, and I let out an unintentional squeak. I'd let him do anything . . .

Except that.

"No!" I have never had anyone inside me that way. Not my husband. Not anyone. Lex has already gotten so many parts of me. He doesn't need that too. I shake my head.

"Rabbit," he says more sternly. "Don't I always make you feel good?"

"No. I can think of a few times you didn't." He's done plenty of things that didn't make me feel good . . . or didn't make me feel good at first.

"What if we play a game? I'll let you run, and if I catch you, I'm taking your ass."

My mind flashes to when he ate my pussy on the hood after he caught me. How hard he made me come. God, I want *that*, but I don't want what he's offering now. I don't want him to fuck my ass.

"No, Lex," I say in a firm voice that won't waver.

"No isn't an answer because it wasn't really a question, Selena." He releases me from his grasp. "But I'll give you a head start."

He kisses me, and it feels like a goodbye. My worry shifts from him taking my ass to him chasing me off to leave me. That idea makes me more scared than being held beneath the water. It makes my stomach clench and my heart gallop.

"When the wolf growls, the bunny runs." Lex leans close to me. Cold water drips from my hair and mingles with his warm breath, creating the perfect storm against my neck. He growls in my ear, sending a vibration through my body. "Run."

I stay planted where I stand, with the lake's rocky bottom beneath my feet.

His eyes narrow and he begins to count. "Ten . . ." He smirks. "Nine . . ."

I draw a sharp breath. He isn't joking. I can see the seriousness all over his face. He ticks down the seconds, giving me less time to get away from him. This is his little hunting game. Well, I guess it was mine first, but it has much higher stakes this time.

This game will hurt.

I turn and head for the shore, but the weight of the water slows every step. It's like moving through a nightmare, only I won't wake up when his fingers grasp my skin. Sharp rocks dig into my feet with each step I take. I ignore the pain. What he has in store for me will make these rocks feel like walking on cotton balls. I'm already winded by the time I reach the bank. He slowly walks behind me, still counting down. His usually pleasant voice becomes ominous as each number leaves his lips.

I scan the terrain, trying to adjust to the foreign surroundings. The only light to be found is from the glow of the sun just breaking the horizon. A path loops around the lake, and I bolt toward it. The soil is wet with dew, and my feet sink into the earth. It's cold mush between my toes. Embedded stones cut at my feet, and I try to ignore the pain. I have to keep going.

I can't hear him behind me anymore. I can only hear my feet pounding against the path. I run toward the trees, using the thick trunks to steady myself as I climb up a hill. I don't have time to think about my nakedness or my healing bruises. I don't even register the branches thwacking against my skin. None of that will matter if his hungry hands catch me.

At the top of the hill, I lean over to catch my breath, scanning the direction I came from. I can't see Lex, and I again worry he's done all this just to leave me, that he's run me off like a dog he doesn't want anymore. This thought hurts more than the sharp stab I feel in my side with each breath I take.

A raindrop splatters on my arm, and I look up at the sky.

Lightning cuts the waning darkness above me before the sky opens and the rain falls in a steady downpour. Fantastic. The drops roll over my skin and ice my bones. They travel over my chest and chill my breasts, hardening my nipples. I wrap my arms around myself to warm them.

"Rabbit?" Lex calls out, and I whip my head toward his voice. I spin on my heels and take off again toward a small pond surrounded by large rocks. The rain cuts across my eyes, blinding me. I blow it from my lips as I run. Just as I reach the first large rock, Lex pops up from beside it.

"God, I know you," he growls.

I dodge his grasp and take off around the pond. My lungs burn, and it feels like there's not enough air in the world to satisfy my need for oxygen. My heart races, thumping against my chest almost painfully. A sharp rock cuts my ankle, and I limp a few steps before the adrenaline helps me forget the pain.

My thoughts are wrapped up in Lex.

In my mind's eye he looks like a predator, transforming into an actual wolf in front of me. I imagine his paws moving the earth as he runs after me. I'm the rabbit, using sheer speed to keep ahead of his gnashing jaws.

I stop at the tree line and turn, looking back as I lean against a tree to catch my breath. There is no sound. Nothing but the patter of heavy rain. He can easily hide his steps beneath that sound. I can't see anything through the thick raindrops, and blinking does nothing to clear the haze collecting around my eyelashes.

The rain is relentless, just like Lex.

"I don't want to play anymore, Lex!" I yell to nothingness.

An arm wraps around my waist from behind, and I scream out. A hand covers my mouth.

"Got you," Lex snarls against my ear.

He presses his chilled, wet body against me, and I whimper into his hand. He keeps his arm around my waist and pushes me toward a large rock. He bends me over it, running his hands along my arms until he can grip my wrists and put them out in front of me, dropping my chest to the cold, slick stone.

"I've never let myself be fully selfish with your body," he whispers, "but right now, the wolf is going to be a wolf." He drops his hand from my mouth.

"Lex," I say with a shake of my head.

"Shh, rabbit." He comforts me for a moment by running his hands over my sides. I feel the grit of mud on my skin. "Do you trust me?"

I swallow. His hard cock presses against my ass. "I have to," I whisper.

"Yes, you do."

The rain patters against me and drips down the pebbled skin of my back. I tremble, not only from the cold but from fear of the pain he'll cause me.

He surprises me when he pushes inside my pussy, and I gasp as he presses my pelvis against the rough rock in front of me. He fucks me with the selfishness he promised. Hard and rough. Rougher than I've ever felt. He rips through me. A feral groan leaves his lips, and that sound embeds itself in my pussy as much as his cock does. His fingers dig into the flesh of my hips, and I'm exactly where I need to be. Both of us are. We're living in a moment where rain washes away our sins and makes us pure.

We are one.

With his cock still buried deep inside me, he spreads my ass, rubbing his finger along my skin before pushing it inside me. I clench, and it makes him moan. "Relax," he says as he slips another finger inside me. And a third, working me up to his cock. I kind of like how full it makes me feel to have his fingers inside me while his cock is in my pussy.

Lex pulls his fingers out, spreads me, and spits. I bite my lip as his warm saliva mixes with the cold rain. He leans over me, and my ass nestles against the crook of his pelvis.

"You ready?" he asks.

I didn't expect him to ask. He *knows* I'm not ready. I'll never be ready for this. My body thought it had a choice for a moment, but I tense all over again when I realize this was never the case.

"Lex . . ."

He drops his hands to either side of my head, leaning his weight onto me. "Don't say my name like that. I won fair and square, bunny. Your ass is mine."

I want to give him that part of me, but I'm scared. He pulls out of my pussy and draws his hips back to get a better angle. As he pushes the head of his cock inside me, I tense. It isn't like his fingers. It feels nothing like his fingers.

"Remember what I said to do. Relax," he whispers as he strokes wet hair from my cheek. "Let me inside, bunny."

His smooth words make me melt into the granite. I take a deep breath and try to relax my body. He inches further inside me, and I bite my lower lip. He's hardly the selfish wolf he claimed he'd be, too tender to be a predator.

"Good fucking girl," he groans as he pushes himself inside me. He keeps his hips still, allowing me to adjust to his size and stretch around him. "You take everything I give you, don't you?" His words mimic what he said in the car when I took his spit. Now, with him this deep inside me, I want to take everything he can give me.

To make him proud.

I whimper and nod. His thrusts grow hungrier, and the

gentleness dissolves. His left hand grips the rock so he can get more leverage. He fucks me harder, but not as hard as when he was in my pussy. The leaves of the trees melt into the ground along with their big, strong trunks. The pond in front of me spreads and takes over everything, blanketing it in blackness. The world becomes abstract, and the only thing that remains real is Lex and his body against mine.

"You feel so fucking good, bunny. So tight. So goddamn perfect."

His words warm me until I only feel the heat of him. It's a fire burning behind me, erasing the cold rain and brisk air. I get used to the pain of him inside me. It never goes away, but I adapt to the hurt like I did with my marriage.

He fucks me harder and deeper, and I feel his full strength for the first time. I feel the selfish hunger he promised me. He uses me as if this is all I'm good for.

My body remains rigid no matter how hard I try to relax. My muscles ache for release. He finally notices that my clenched jaw isn't from the chattering of my teeth. He becomes aware of the tense tremble of pain in my body and transforms back into the Lex I know. He leans over and kisses my shoulder. It's a tender touch I need so badly at this moment. I need it more than my next breath.

"Sweet bunny," he whispers. "I'll stop."

"No!" I cry out. "I want to take everything you give me."

He chuckles, but it turns into a growl at the end. "You have, Selena. You really fucking have. This was a lot for anyone to take. The chase. The rain and the bloody cuts on your feet and ankles. Taking my cock in your ass with nothing more than my spit and the wetness of your cunt. You're such a good girl. Even when your body isn't willing, your mind is."

"I'm sorry," I say as I fight back tears. The prospect of

disappointing him incites more emotion than most anything in my life has.

His hand glides down the curve of my spine. "Don't apologize. I wanted to fuck your ass, and I needed you to let me. And you did." He grips my ass, and the rain makes his fingertips bite harder. "You won't like everything I want to do to you, that I *will* do to you, but I'll always reward you for being the good girl you are. No matter how bad you become from being around me, you're my good fucking girl."

He pulls out of me and lifts me to my feet. His mouth finds mine as he lays me back on the rock and spreads my thighs. His lips trail down my body, and he drops to his knees. They sink into the earth. He parts me, and his tongue finds my clit. I lift myself onto my elbows so I can watch him. He tosses back his wet hair as rainwater drips down his temples. Droplets of rain roll over the muscles in his arms and shoulders.

My eyes wash over his prison-etched tattoos, and I realize he's someone my family wouldn't have allowed me to talk to, let alone fuck. I'm in over my head with him. Way over my head. He's an enigma, a mystery that should be left unsolved and untouched, yet he eats my pussy like the answers to all I need to know are in his mouth. He selfishly fucks me with his tongue, his hands gripping my ass as he holds me at his mercy.

"Lex," I whisper.

"Don't say my name unless the words 'I'm coming' follow it," he growls, giving me a dark look before devouring me again. His commands, like always, make me weak. Make me tremble as his words vibrate my clit.

When he realizes his harsh words made me buck

against his mouth, his voice lowers "Come for me, bunny. Get off to the one man you shouldn't."

And I do. I come hard against his mouth, with the rain painting my body and the trees crawling up from the earth and surrounding us once more. I grip his hair as he relentlessly tongues my clit, making my body shudder with a pleasure that morphs into discomfort. He smirks up at me and swipes my clit once more, my body jolting from his touch, before he rises to his feet.

The rock rakes my soft skin as I sit up. "What about you?" I ask, feeling guilty as my orgasm wanes.

His broad frame towers over me, and water cascades down his firm chest and stomach. "What about me?"

"You didn't come." I feel bad that I tapped out before he could get his release, but Lex seems relaxed, satiated almost, despite not coming at all.

He reaches out and helps me to my feet. "It's fine, bunny. I'll fill you up the first chance I get." His eyes scan the horizon. "We'll take another quick dip and then we gotta get going. It's morning."

I nod. I have no idea what will happen to us, but Lex is opening me up to a world I never knew existed. One where the risk of losing my freedom is the most freedom I've ever felt.

Chapter Fifteen

Selena

I t feels like it's getting more and more rural the further south we go. There's so much farm country in Tennessee, and I can't help but get lost in the sight. Small homesteads with various livestock line the road on both sides. Cows, goats, and some horses stand in a large paddock, and I press my forehead to the glass to take them all in.

Lex takes a right-hand turn, and we follow along the fancy wooden fences. I don't know what Lex has planned as we drive down yet another secluded dead-end road. The eternity of pavement feels endless. We drove for a long time today, and we're both worn down. He just won't admit it. I will, with a long exhale.

"Where are we going?" I ask.

"We need a new car. When I got gas, I overheard two locals talking about a lonely farmer who lives up this road. Said he was away, and it sounded like a good opportunity. An easy one."

I tighten my lips and rub the cuts on my ankles. "I need to wash these with actual soap." Natural water sources aren't hygienic. Not in the slightest. I *need* a real shower.

"You will." Lex's eyes jump to a rickety farmhouse ahead of us. "There it is, just like they said."

Lex pulls to the side of the road, and we walk the last bit toward the house. My feet ache from my shoes rubbing everywhere the rocks and branches bit my skin.

"What happened to your biological parents?" I ask, trying to distract myself from my pain by hearing his.

Lex doesn't speak at first. I don't expect him to answer my question, but he surprises me when he does. "Never met my father and hardly knew my mother. She liked dope better than me. I've been in and out of the foster system since they found me alone in an apartment surrounded by needles when I was six."

"Lex—"

"Don't, rabbit. I hear the pity in your voice." He shakes his head. "We all can't be as lucky as you were growing up."

I stop mid-step and turn toward him. He doesn't need to attack me because he's hurt. He doesn't have to get so defensive. "You know nothing about how I grew up."

"Don't I?"

I scoff. "No. You don't. I hardly knew my parents, either. They threw money at me to make up for being absent. I had one purpose as their daughter, and it was to marry whoever would better their business. They handed me to the devil even though they knew they were sending me to hell with him. They *knew* he'd burn me. Money has kept me alive while simultaneously killing me. I'd give it all up, and I have. There's no more beyond what I took, and I'm fine with it." My shoulders drop from the weight of the finality of my life before Lex. I still wouldn't take anything back.

"Selena," Lex says as I quicken my steps toward the house.

I ignore him. When he keeps trying, I turn on my heels and narrow my eyes at him. "You think I'm a spoiled little brat, don't you? Fancy fucking show rabbit, right? Too special to get it dirty or allow it to be an animal. I've tried to show you that I'm not some fragile, well-groomed little thing!"

Lex raises his voice in a way I've never heard directed at me. "Selena, you need to calm the hell down. Where is this even coming from?"

It's coming from him. The things he says about my life make me so angry. I see the way he looks at me sometimes, like I'm some spoiled brat who ran away from a perfect life. It's a deep-seated insecurity from always being told my life was fine because I had money and nice things. When I told my mother what Bryce was doing to me, she said, "But he's supporting you, Selena. I know how you can be. Sometimes you just need to change your behavior a bit to make him happy." Because he "supported" me, I had to accept the pain. *I* had to change, not the one inflicting the abuse. Fuck Lex for thinking I was somehow shielded from pain because of fucking money.

No, it was the root of all evil in my family and my marriage.

The weight of it crushes me, and I lose the strength to hold myself up. I fall to my knees. Lex runs to help me up, but I push his hands away. "Let me be for a few minutes. The house is right there. I'll meet you inside."

Lex shakes his head and looks up at the farmhouse. "I'm not leaving you out here alone."

"That's precisely what I need right now. I need to be alone," I whisper. I sit back on my heels and breathe in the heavy farm air. It smells like grain and manure. A tear slips down my cheek, and I wipe it away before he can see it. I don't need him to stay and comfort me. I need to comfort myself.

"Selena," he commands, but for once I don't listen.

"Go!" I yell back, surprising myself with the ferocity.

Lex draws a breath and reaches for the knife in his pocket. "Just in case a different wolf tries to bite." He tosses it toward me and it lands in front of me, flattening the grass. It brings back a rush of memories. The way my hand concealed the intricately carved wooden handle. The way the blade blossomed red as I stabbed Bryce over and over again.

Once Lex leaves to go inside, I drop onto my butt and lie down. A broad-winged bird soars overhead, silent and menacing. Cows moo in the pasture beside the house. It's pretty fucking peaceful, and I need this peace. I wish Lex understood. I don't want to fight with him over our pasts. I don't want to participate in a competition about who had the worst childhood. Clearly he did, but it doesn't negate what happened to me. And I feel negated. We chose different paths—I chose complacency, and he chose violence—but we both chose murder, and that's where our paths cross.

Something crashes inside the house. I wipe a rogue tear from the crease of my eyes and get to my feet. I pluck the knife from the grass and grip it against my palm. When I get to the porch, I creep up the steps and open the door, controlling it as it closes so it doesn't make any noise. The crashing grows louder and more violent. It can't possibly be coming from Lex alone. With quiet footfalls, I follow the loud noises to the living room.

What I see surprises me. A burly farmer has Lex in the same hold Lex held Rodney in, but this fight isn't nearly as one-sided. My mouth gapes because after everything I've witnessed, I would never expect someone to get the upper hand on Lex. The farmer's hat falls off as the men wrestle. Greasy strands of hair fall over the man's face. His overalls are ripped and stained.

When Lex catches my eyes for a moment, he mouths, "*Go*," to me. I shake my head, never more certain of anything in my life. There's no way I'm leaving him to save myself.

My heart thumps in my ears as Lex tries to stay in the fight. His pistol glints in the back of his jeans, but I'll never be fast enough to get to it, nor would I know what to do with it if I managed to get my hands on it.

In my panic, I forget about the knife in my hand. Its weight against my palm finally reminds me of its presence. I slink along the wall, trying to keep the farmer from seeing me. When I accidentally knock over a can of beer, I hold my breath, expecting him to hear. Thankfully, no one hears a damn thing over the grunting and adrenaline. Once I'm flat against the wall behind the farmer, I open the blade and hold it within a familiar grasp. I have no idea how to stab this man, though. I don't even know if I can. Vengeance propelled my arm when it came to Bryce, but there's no vengeance now. There's only the need to protect Lex, and those are two very different reasons for killing.

Fear freezes me in place. I don't know what to do.

The farmer goes for the gun, and I'm out of time to think. The intense need to protect Lex propels my arm forward as I rush for the farmer and sink the knife into his neck. He lets out a roar, and I squeal as blood streams from beneath the handle.

"Pull it out, Selena! Pull the knife out!" Lex yells, and it sounds like he's miles away.

With my hand still wrapped around the handle, I try to tug it out, but a suction that wasn't there when I put it in holds it in place. I wiggle it and it finally gives way with a disgusting squelching sound. The moment the blade leaves his neck, blood escapes the wound in a waterfall, spurting a geyser of crimson with every beat of his heart. The man wobbles on his feet and reaches for his neck. Lex pulls away and rips his pistol from the farmer's hand, putting it in his waistband where it belongs.

It feels like minutes, but it's merely seconds before the farmer crashes to his knees. Without uttering another sound, he falls onto his face. I've never seen so much blood. Every bit of what was in his body spreads around him on the floor.

"Arterial wound. Very fucking effective, rabbit," Lex pants. He's covered in blood, and my arms are sprayed with it, too.

The bleeding I caused.

I back against the wall, the knife still in my trembling hand. As if Lex forgot what murder feels like to unseasoned killers, he doesn't seem to notice the anguish I'm facing. My stomach churns and I heave, nearly throwing up all over the old hardwood floors. Lex grabs my hair and holds it for me as I fight back the vomit. He rubs my back like he's comforting someone who bowled a bad game. How can he be so cavalier?

It's selective of me to forget who Lex really is. It's too

easy to ignore the violent and dangerous side of him that seems as normal as breathing to him.

I stand, feeling the weight of that giant farmer on my shoulders. How will I carry that with me? My eyes widen with fear, not of Lex, but of what I've become because of him.

A killer.

I'm not just a battered wife who got revenge. I'm a full-blown fucking murderer.

"It gets easier," Lex says as he pats my back. He strolls toward the cabinet and starts rooting around. My mouth drops open. He is fucking clinical. Literally sociopathic.

"Easier?" I ask, disgusted.

"Yeah, easier. Meaning you don't get all worked up about it anymore."

I blink at him. "You are fucking insane, Lex."

He closes a cabinet and begins to eat from a bag of chips, bloody hands and all. "Yeah, and?"

Anger courses through me. He's maddening. "You made me do that!" I scream as I point at the dead farmer, quickly cutting my gaze when it lands on his fixed eyes, the life drained from them.

Lex laughs through a mouthful of chips. "I didn't make you do a damn thing," he says with an infuriating calmness. "I told you to go. You had the choice to leave."

He walks closer, pushes me against the wall, and wrangles the knife from my hand. His breath rolls over my heated skin. "I didn't make you fuck me or stab your husband. I didn't make you come with me or stab that man. If you're going to stay with me, you need to start accepting what you are."

"And what the hell am I?"

Lex flashes his darkened eyes at me. "You're no better than me."

I draw a sharp breath, as if he's stabbed me beneath my ribs. The air deflates from my lungs, and I shrink in front of him. "I just wanted to protect you . . ." I whisper.

Lex leans in, and I flinch against his touch as he kisses my forehead. "You already knew I'd kill for you, and now I know you'll kill for me." Lex drops his mouth to mine and kisses me once before running a hot hand up my throat. "And as sexy as it is, don't ever ignore me again when I tell you to leave."

"But—"

"But nothing, rabbit. If I tell you to go, you go. Do you hear me? If he'd killed me, what would he have done to a girl like you, huh? If it were me? Shit. I'd have fucked you half to death out of principle. So I need you to listen to me, Selena. For once in your fucking life."

Lex

Stubborn goddamn rabbit. I breathe in her scent as I scold her. I'm not a piece of shit. I appreciate her saving my life, but not at the risk of her own. A shiver dances up my spine at the thought of what would've happened to her if he shot me and turned to face her.

Beautiful little bunny, ripe for slaughter.

I imagine him fucking her, tearing her apart in ways I couldn't bring myself to do despite *really* wanting to. I force away the intrusive thoughts of his hands on what's mine. I can't handle the thought of his mouth on her plump lips or pale neck. His eyes all over her tits and his fingers touching her perfect cunt.

The thoughts alone make me homicidal.

My hands ride up her neck and grip her face. The weight of the risk of her being with me begins to bury me. To suffocate me. This is why I wanted her to stay back in her idyllic home where she was safe. I can protect her if I'm not gravely injured or dead. I'm certain of that. But what would happen once I can't protect her anymore?

If something happens to me.

If my rabbit becomes prey to someone else.

"If you can't promise you'll listen when I tell you something, I'll leave you at the nearest bus stop," I say as I drop my forehead to hers.

"Lex," she whispers in soft protest.

"Promise me!"

"I promise," she finally whispers.

"Atta girl," I say as I pull her into my chest.

"You're bleeding." She dabs at my shirt. I lift it and see that my cut is oozing again.

"It's nothing. Probably from the fight." I draw away from her and go to the bathroom to find some bandages. After I dress the wound, I return to the living room. Selena has seated herself on the couch after covering the farmer's body with a sheet.

"How are you so unbothered?" she asks without looking back at me.

"I'll let you in on a little secret," I say as I walk up behind her and grip her hair in a fist. "I'm a documented sociopath. A convicted killer." I lean down and kiss her neck as she fights against my touch. She tries to pull away, but I hold her there. She isn't strong enough to escape my hold.

"You aren't making this better," she snaps.

"But I'm not making it worse, either," I say through a smirk against her skin. "I'm a killer and so are you. There's no arguing away the blood on our hands, no rationalizing that it was our upbringing or a lapse in sanity. We made the conscious decision to rip away someone's life. We made our bed, and now we'll fuck in it."

I crane her neck and kiss her throat, completely unbothered by the blood painting her skin. In fact, I like it. I love that she's covered in his blood. That she killed for *me*. I lick at the crimson, enjoying the metallic taste on my tongue, and her body tenses in disgust. As my licking becomes a soft bite on her neck, she relaxes. The softest moan, hardly audible, rolls off her lower lip.

"Speaking of beds, I fucked up the last time we were in one. What do you say we take advantage of the one here? Give me a chance to fuck you right. Like you deserve."

Despite enjoying my touch for a moment, her eyes snap to mine. "No, Lex, absolutely not. There's a dead man on the ground behind us."

"Oh, rabbit, must we make it another game? Something new for me to do to you?"

She narrows her eyes. "No."

"Well, go take a shower while I take care of this, and I'll figure out what game I want to play with you."

The call to shower is too enticing for her, and like a scared animal, she leaves the room without turning her back to me, as if I'll pounce on her if she isn't watching.

Believe me, I'm tempted to. I'd love to fuck her with the farmer's blood still on her skin. Unfortunately, dealing with the body is my job to do.

I turn him over and stare at his vacant eyes. *Poor bastard,* I think as I roll him up in the sheet. He had gotten the rare upper hand on me. I didn't expect him to be home.

Like an idiot, I hadn't even considered it. Had I been alone, I would have been done for. And I probably deserved it. Then again, if I'd been alone, I wouldn't have been in the farmer's house, and he wouldn't be dead.

My course of action has shifted with Selena involved. If it had just been me, I'd have taken her car and driven straight to the border. With her in tow, I need to give her a comfortable place to sleep every night and keep her fed, fucked, and happy. I desperately want to keep her safe, which is why I wanted to get a new vehicle for us in the first place. That landed us on this poor sap's doorstep.

I wipe my forehead. My fingers work to tie off the sheet toward his feet, then I drag the body outside. The rickety screen door slams. I haul his body behind the house, near the Bilco doors that open to the basement. I cover him with a tarp and stick the shovel over it as if there's nothing but a pile of mulch beneath it. I'll fully deal with that later—when I'm not so sexually frustrated.

I rub my hand on my jeans, smearing the blood. I enter the house and eye the pool of red on the floor. There's far too much to clean. The wood has sucked it into every crevice, every pore. I look around for a rug instead. When I see the one under the coffee table, I tug it out and lay it over the bloody mess. It hides nearly all of it. Out of sight, out of mind—for Selena, at least. I would have fucked her on that couch with or without his body there. Let his soul watch me make her come.

My shirt sticks to my sweaty skin. I follow the sounds of the shower until I reach a rundown hallway door. When I reach for the knob, it's locked. "Sneaky rabbit," I whisper.

She needs to stop trying to lock me out. Hasn't she learned she can't keep me out of anything? Not the room, her heart, *or* her cunt.

The slit in the lock is easy to turn with just my knife. When I open the door, I stare at her naked body through the shower's dingy glass. Arching her back to wash her hair, she doesn't notice me at first. I adjust the front of my pants and watch her. Knowing the blood washing off her body is the life-force of the man she killed for me makes me hard as fuck. The way she stabbed him and listened to me when I told her to rip it from his flesh . . . God, I have never seen a more beautiful act. In the same breath, I feel more guilt for changing her into something she wasn't before meeting me.

I've never felt guilt, nor true remorse, until I met her. I hate seeing pieces of myself in Selena. Her good pieces mix with my bad.

The water turns off, and when she opens the door, she jumps. "Jesus, how'd you get in here?" she asks. By now she should know that nothing can keep me from her when I want her.

I shake the knife in my hand and set it on the countertop. "Get back in there, rabbit."

She reaches for a raggedy towel, but I yank it across the bar and out of reach. "Why? I'm done."

"Maybe. But I'm not," I tell her with a smirk, unwilling to hide how hard I am from watching her. I slip off my shoes and unzip my jeans. Her gaze rolls downward and locks on my hard cock. I slip off my bloody shirt and let it fall beside my pants.

"Lex, I'm not in the mood," she whispers.

"But I am," I say with a growl. I pull the shower door open the rest of the way and run my gaze over her naked body. Without taking my eyes off her, I turn the shower on again. She looks scared and small, like when I first fucked her. That farmer's gotten to her, which means she's still more human than I can ever be.

Good.

I drag her into the shower with me. I lean back and let the hot water rain down on me, taking the blood with it. When I hear the shower door open again, I reach out and grab her waist. "You aren't leaving like that," I say.

"Like what?"

"Scared."

She scoffs. "I'm not scared of you."

I draw her against my body. "I know you aren't scared of me. You're scared of yourself. Afraid of what you're capable of." I kiss her, but her lips don't welcome me like they usually do. "You're capable of anything, rabbit. You can be the sweet woman who softens me and the unsavory—sometimes homicidal—little rabbit that hardens me."

She draws a sharp breath that leaves me wondering if I offended her. As she tries to pull away from me, I realize I have. I let her out of my grasp to pin her against the shower wall.

"Stop, Selena. Stop fucking running from what you are when you never ran from what I am. You have darkness inside you, whether it's in here"—I graze her chest before lowering my hand to her pussy—"or in here."

Her eyes roll up my chest, and she pushes out her lower lip. The tension in her body melts away, and I step back to finish washing the blood from my skin.

"What's going to happen to us?" she asks. She's so quiet I almost don't hear her over the water.

"Nothing, Selena. I won't let anything happen to us. Do you trust me?"

"Not really." Her lips tick up in a small smile.

"Yes you do, bunny," I say as I drag her into me and kiss her again.

She meets my affection this time. I reach back and pull

the showerhead off the holder. I turn it to a more focused stream and run it along her body, sending the warm water against her hardening nipples. I move it over her stomach before lowering it to her inner thighs. She grips the metal and stops my ascent toward her pussy.

"What? Have you never got yourself off in the shower?" I ask.

She stares at me with a trembling lower lip and shakes her head.

"Please tell me you get yourself off." My tone is almost mocking, but I don't mean for it to be. This girl cannot be *that* innocent.

"With my hand," she says as she looks away.

"So you've never used any kind of toy?" I ask.

She shakes her head once more, and I remove the showerhead from her hand. I grab her wrists and pin them above her head. She struggles within my grasp, her back arching as she tries to pull away. I put my knee between her legs and spread them.

"Stay open for me," I tell her. I keep both wrists encased in one hand as I run the showerhead down her body once more and aim it at the soft mound of hair between her legs. Her eyes clench shut, and I let her keep them closed.

I palm the back of the showerhead and slip deeper between her legs. The moment the stream parts her lips and washes over her clit, she lurches forward, nearly ripping her hands from my grasp.

"How does that feel, sweet bunny?" I ask as I hold the pressure between her legs. Every so often I stroke her with the stream, moving it in a small circle.

"It feels good," she whispers. A moan leaves her lips, and she bucks her hips forward.

"Keep your hands against that wall." I release her and

wrap my hand around my cock. I stroke myself to her grinding against the showerhead. I focus on my head as she moans and whimpers. "Open your eyes," I command. I want to see her looking up at me. I want to see the pleasure lighting her eyes on fire.

She does, but she doesn't look me in the face. Her eyes drop to my hand on my cock. With a deep, passionate kiss, I stroke my dick against her lower stomach and keep the water aimed at her clit. Her hips curl against me and she moans, getting me too close. I stop myself before I come, taking my hand away from my dick for a moment.

I lift my fingers to her face and trace her jaw. "You have the sweetest face, bunny. Do you know what I want to do to you?"

She shakes her head and swallows.

"I want to paint your skin with my come." My fingers graze her chin and cheeks. "Did your husband ever come on your face?"

She shakes her head. "No." The word comes out with a frustrated buck of her hips.

"Would you let me?" I ask.

I expect an instant no—it's probably too demeaning for a girl like her—but she surprises me with a slow, unsure nod. Her building orgasm must have made her more pliable.

"Tell me with your words, bunny. You know I like to hear it."

She moans and her thighs tremble. "I want you to come on my face, Lex."

The way she says my name at the end makes me twitch against her stomach. I want that so goddamn bad, and hearing her ask is nearly enough to make me come without touching myself.

"Come, sweet bunny," I tell her as I stroke myself again.

She leans back against the wall and closes her eyes. She drops her hands, and as much as I want to scold her for it, they land on my shoulders, digging her pleasure into me through her fingertips. I allow it because I need to feel it too.

"Talk to me. Tell me how it feels."

Selena digs her fingers deeper as she bucks her hips. "I'm gonna come, Lexington," she moans.

I hate my full name . . . except when she says it.

"Come for me so I can put you on your knees, sweet bunny."

I rub my cock, fighting the urge to come as her body ripples with her orgasm. She trembles, screaming out in pleasure and grabbing my hand to pull the showerhead away as she gets too sensitive. I keep my hand there, letting the water wash over her spasming clit.

"Stop," she begs.

I lean in and kiss her. "Ride it out to the end," I groan against her mouth.

And she does. Like the good girl she is, she rides out the earthquakes of pleasure ripping through her. She rides out the pain as I keep the pressure on her clit after she comes.

"Get on your knees," I say, knowing my release is coming. I feel it in the base of my balls, and I try to slow my strokes to hold out for her.

I stare at her, following her with my eyes as she drops to her knees. Her gaze meets mine, her large eyes looking up at me with satiated desire. There's a hint of fear there, too. Fear of something new. Something her husband never did to her.

I release my cock and let it settle in front of her face. I'm so tempted to push it between her full lips, but then I'd come in her mouth. My hand grazes her cheek as the other pushes her dark hair away from her face.

"I want you to keep your eyes on me. I don't want you to close them for even a second, even as I spill my come on your face." I stop stroking her cheek and stroke my cock instead. "Talk to me, bunny."

"I want your come, Lex," she whispers.

I growl. "You're mine, Selena. You know that, right?" My abdomen tightens. She looks so obedient at my feet. Her hands grasp the outsides of my thighs as she keeps her eyes on my face.

"I'm yours," she whispers, and I rub my thumb along her lower lip.

I grab the back of her head, ball her hair in my fist, and crane her neck just a bit more so I can see her pout over my cock. I touch the tip to her mouth, grazing the seam of her lips. I stop stroking my head, only jerking off the shaft so I can see it all. All that I need to give her. Her warm lips rest against the tip of my dick, and it's enough to make me come whether I stroke myself or not.

"I'm gonna come," I growl.

Pearls of white shoot from me, and just like I demanded, she doesn't even blink as my come hits her cheek. It spills over her mouth as I rub it against her soft, warm skin. She looks so fucking beautiful covered in my come.

I help her to her feet and wipe some of my come from her mouth before pushing it past her lips and onto her tongue. "Taste me, bunny."

Her lips tighten around my fingers. She doesn't like the taste, but she still moves her mouth up to my fingertips. I growl. I don't care that I still coat her lips and tongue. I lean in and kiss her. She whimpers against my mouth.

"Goddamn it, rabbit," I whisper as I bite her lower lip, taking in the salty taste mixed with the sweetness of her mouth.

I grab the showerhead again, turn it on a softer setting, and tell her to put her head back. I wash my come from her perfect face, and she wipes at her cheeks beneath the stream. The window above the shower sends a halo of light onto the wall above her head. She looks angelic, and it's the closest I'll ever get to an angel.

Chapter Sixteen

Selena

I feel like we're playing house in some alternate universe where it's perfectly normal that Lex just came in from disposing of a body. With dirt still on his hands, he walks toward me, wraps his hands around my face, and draws me in for a hard kiss. The scents of soil and decay cling to his flesh. His hand moves behind my head, and he pulls me into him as he strokes my hair. I feel like a child against him. His strong, overbearing frame feels safe. No matter how safe he makes me feel in that moment, I still find myself longing for stability again.

Lex's body tenses. Heavy footsteps plod across the old wooden porch.

"Richard?" calls the voice on the other side of the door.

Very different expressions cross our faces. For me, it's wide-eyed fear. For him, it's narrowing anger. We freeze, and my heart races in my chest. Despite the haze of fear descending on my mind, I think of something that might work. It may just save us. Well, save whoever is out there and keep another death from weighing on my conscience.

"I have an idea. Go anywhere else," I tell Lex.

"I don't like this," he says with a shake of his head, posturing toward the door with his pistol clutched in his hand. I'm tempted to let him take care of the unexpected visitor, but my guilt from the farmer's death still lingers in my chest.

"Go," I tell him with a firm rise in my voice.

His eyes narrow before he disappears through the kitchen. I stroke my fingers through my unbrushed hair and go to the door, where a stocky young guy waits on the other side.

"Who're you? And where's Richard?"

"I'm his niece. He's gone for a little while. Told me to stay and watch the farm."

The man raises an eyebrow. "You're Lana? You don't look like no farm girl from Nebraska."

"Well, I am," I snap. I don't intend to, but the accusation on his face rubs me the wrong way, even if he has every reason to be suspicious.

He pulls out his phone. "I'm gonna call Richard. Something doesn't smell right." He's not wrong about that, but I'm certain he can't smell the scent of death because it's all in my head.

I take a subtle breath, trying to remain as calm as I can. I know what happens when men sense my fear. They prey on it. Even Lex.

"If you do that, the stubborn old thing will come right back home. Do you know how hard it was to get him to leave in the first place?"

The man lowers his phone. "Yeah, I guess he needed to get away. He was going crazy all alone out here." He leans in and peers inside, his tone shifting as much as his body. "You all by your lonesome, too? Big ol' house for just one girl." He rubs a thick hand through a scraggly black beard.

My tightening stomach fires a warning shot through my body. It's a familiar feeling.

"Well, I best be going," I tell him as I try to close the door.

He puts his hand out to keep me from closing the door, and I nearly slam it on his thick fingers. "Oh, don't be like that. We're just talking," he says.

With a motion too swift for me to react to, he tugs me out by my arm and puts his big hand over my mouth. He even covers my nose, and soon my lungs beg for air. Unlike every time Lex has done something similar, there's an instant panic that drains the pent-up oxygen and makes my body lurch with need from the start. I feel like I'm suffocating.

Dying.

"You ain't his niece," the man says with a snarl. "His kin don't look like you." He pins my chest against the house, and his hand rides up my thigh over my leggings. "God-damn, if you were *my* niece, I'd be tempted to put you on my lap."

My stomach clenches until I feel like I'm going to vomit. With his hand covering my nose and mouth, I couldn't, even if I wanted to. I'm trapped in this pervert's predatory grasp.

I should have listened to Lex.

Tears slip down my cheeks. The hand over my face moves down and lets me draw in several panicked breaths through my nose. His other hand goes down the front of my pants. More tears fall.

"Fuck," he groans. "That's a pussy like we ain't have

165

around here." His hot tobacco-laced breath rushes over my neck.

I don't see or hear Lex walking along the side of the house until he's in my vision's periphery. He crouches, holds the pistol, and aims. There's no way he'll miss me if he aims at the man's head when it's so close to mine.

He seems to realize this and lowers the barrel. Lex shoots once, and the sound of squelching flesh erupts behind me as the deafening boom makes my ears ring. The man stumbles back, clutching his side. He looks shocked as he wordlessly holds the wound, blood spreading around his fingers.

Lex takes aim once more and puts a bullet through the man's face, taking him down in a bloody spray of brain matter along the porch. I throw my hands over my ears and fall back against the house. Lex runs to me, but I can't hear what he's saying over the ringing in my ears. He lifts me to my feet and drags me inside.

"Selena!" He smacks my cheek, cupping it the last time. He pulls me into his chest, but that safe feeling is gone.

Completely gone.

My ears begin to clear, the residual ringing becoming quieter until it's nearly gone. I don't register what's happening, but Lex sits on the couch and places me on his lap. I turn my head to nestle into his neck, and he lets me for a moment before making me look at him. His eyes glisten with a show of concern I haven't seen from him before. Not as Rodney tried to do what he did or when Bryce went even further.

"I'm so sorry," he whispers as he brushes back my hair. "That's why I didn't like your idea, rabbit. If something happened, I knew you'd be in the crossfire. I had no choice but to go around the house so I could get a shot off without hitting you, which meant he had you in his grasp longer than I would have ever allowed."

"I just wanted to get rid of him without hurting anyone else," I whisper.

"This is why this life isn't meant for you. You have to put yourself first and anyone else beneath you." He drops his forehead to mine. "Actually, I'm failing at that, too. I put you above me. Can't even take my own fucking advice. You give me the humanity I don't need or want." He sighs. "But I can't turn back now. Not with you here."

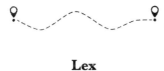

Lex

I'M NOT sure what love is because I've never felt it. My mother never knew what it was, either. I didn't feel a thing when I found my mother dead. I almost felt relieved that she couldn't bring her "friends" over anymore. That I'd stop seeing her railed in front of me.

For my foster parents, love had a price. As long as they kept getting paid, they "loved" me, but only in front of the social workers who checked on me. Jack, an older kid more fucked-up than me, showed me how to survive in the foster system, and it wasn't by feeling things. He showed me how to turn off every part of myself until I was an empty shell, capable of destruction without thought or feelings. People think more about the dirty dish they put in the sink than I do about murdering someone.

Cold. Callous. Deadly.

That's who I was and that's what helped me survive prison.

But Selena is changing that for me. She's reversing conditioning that was perfected long before she was born. I have trauma older than she is.

I hold her close, listening to each ragged breath she takes. My heart breaks for her. That piece of shit violated her, and I couldn't jump right in because I didn't want him to fucking kill her. That's been my fear with bringing her along. She has this look about her—a sweet innocence. When I see that in her, I want to rip her apart and brutalize her. When other men see it, I recognize that same hunger.

Even though I can control that side of me when it comes to her, others can't, and she'll always be at risk of having more of herself stolen away. I can't bring her with me over the border, yet I have no clue how I'll force her to stay back. But I have to. She isn't safe with me, and she wouldn't be safe around the people I would have to put myself around to survive. I'm irrevocably torn between selfishly wanting to keep her or selflessly letting her go to keep her safe.

Her lip pouts and my cock twitches beneath her. I still want to fuck that sweetness out of her and fill her with my darkness. I want to take her until she stops having a heart that beats for anyone but me, until she has no more guilt or regret about the people we kill to keep our hearts beating together.

I grab her chin and kiss her. "How far did he get?" I've been afraid to ask because I don't think I can handle the answer, but I need to know if I'm chopping off the fucker's hands before I bury him.

She shakes her head. "Just got his hand down my pants."

That's one hand I'll chop off and shove in his ass before I put him in the ground for touching her like that.

Her pussy is mine.

I take a deep breath, stopping my barrage of possessive thoughts. I have to let her go. I have to push back my need to own her before we both end up dead or in prison.

"I know you're going to fight me about it, tooth and fucking nail, but you can't stay with me, Selena." I touch her face. "I know you want to, and I want you to as well, but you can't. I thought you had to fear the wolf, but there are bigger predators out there than me. I *have* to keep you safe. It's the one thing I promised myself I'd do, and it's the *one* thing I'm not going back on."

She shakes her head. "Nope, I'm not accepting that bullshit excuse to get rid of me."

"It's not a bullshit excuse, rabbit. Bullshit excuses are what I've been giving myself to justify keeping you with me. None of this is a fucking game. I can't see a scenario with a good end for you, and I don't understand how you can't see that."

I ease her off my lap. Even in my anger, I don't want to hurt her like that. I stand up and tower over her. When I rip my shirt off, I expose a mosaic of mostly prison tattoos—a timeline of violence and hate. I gesture to the bundles of scar tissue on my abdomen and back from the many times I've been stabbed. I'm a mess, not just inside but on the outside.

She can *see* the evil on my body.

"What more of me do you have to see to know you need to run? This isn't safe. I'm not safe." My words bite, but she refuses to recoil.

I grab her by the arm and drag her toward the bedroom. It's old, but at least it has a bed. I sit her down and she looks up at me with those big eyes of hers.

"What do I have to do to make you hate me?"

"There's nothing you can do, Lex," she says in a

maddeningly calm tone despite not knowing the full extent of what I'm capable of. She's seen so much, yet she still seems to forget all she's seen.

"You need to," I snarl. I need her to because I can't hate *her*. If I could, none of this would be so difficult. She'd be dropped off or killed like she means nothing, and I'd be alone by now.

But she means everything.

She folds her arms across her chest defiantly. "Well, I won't."

I climb over her and put a hand to her throat. She whimpers as I squeeze. "What if I took your pussy? What if I tear into you like I've wanted to since the moment I saw you?"

She shakes her head. Her lips tighten, and I know I offended her.

I squeeze her throat harder. "What if I fucked your ass and didn't stop when it made you cry from the pain?"

"No." She strains to get the word out.

Anger rises through me, lighting my skin on fire. She's so fucking naïve to think she'd still enjoy being in my presence if I tore through her the way I want to. I give her a final squeeze, cutting off her air. Her cheeks redden as she reaches for my wrists. Flashes of my foster mother replace her face as I keep my hands around her throat. That anger gets out of control, nearly past the point of stopping myself. I only let go of her throat to turn her onto her stomach, and she hardly flails beneath me as I tug down her leggings.

It pisses me off.

"Hate me, rabbit!" I scream as I unzip my jeans and pull out my cock. I lie over her, pressing the heat of my dick against her bare skin. She whimpers. "Fucking. Hate. Me."

"No," she strains out beneath my weight.

I wrestle with control when I need it the most. I slam my fist beside her head. "Fine. I'm done trying to make it harder than it needs to be. It ends for you here. You aren't coming with me. That's it. There's no arguing about it. There's no more trying to make it easier for you to let me go. I'm taking you to a bus stop." I feel the twist of my stomach with each word.

This is it. For her. For me. For us.

It has to be.

I crawl off her and refuse to look in her eyes. "Get ready to go, Selena."

I wish she understood that I don't have a choice. Neither of us does. I don't deserve someone so stubbornly willing to stay by my side. But I can't keep her. I could never keep her.

Chapter Seventeen

Selena

The loud pickup truck idles nearby as I walk down the long road leading away from the house. It only creeps forward when I get too far ahead. I'm sick of being pushed away. I can make my own decisions and suffer the consequences of my own choices. But he can't understand that.

"Come on, Selena, get in the truck."

"I'm not getting in the truck, Lex. You want me gone, and I won't sit beside you while you get rid of me."

"I'm not letting you walk out here alone. Remember what I said about the predators out here?"

I roll my eyes. "Yeah, there are worse predators than you." I scoff. "I think I'll chance it. Maybe I'll get taken by someone who doesn't have commitment problems."

The truck slams to a halt beside me.

"God, your age is showing. I do *not* have commitment problems."

I swivel on my heels to stare at him, the darkness beginning to wrap around us as the sun goes down. "My age? Fuck you." My steps kick up dust again. The headlights illuminate my back and cast a long shadow in front of me.

"I'm not *fine* with it. But this is what has to happen," he calls over the sound of the engine.

"Then let it happen! *Bye!*" I admit this outburst shows my age, but I don't care anymore. None of it matters. "Don't call yourself a predator when you can't handle your prey."

"I can *handle* my prey just fine. When they fucking listen," he snaps, kicking up dust as he slams on the brakes again.

I laugh. "If you want a compliant woman, I'm a poor choice."

"Were you?"

Oh, fuck him. How dare he throw my past in my face when I've never thrown his at him. Until now. "Real low blow, felon."

I hear a heavy exhale from the truck. "I'm telling you one more time, Selena, get in the fucking truck so I can bring you to the bus station."

I turn toward him. "No."

Lex's jaw ticks as if he's controlling every ounce of what's inside him that wants to punish me.

"How fast can a rabbit run? You want to play games? I'll play too." His voice is low and laced with frustration. His eyes roll up to meet mine, and he becomes the fierce predator once more, transforming in front of my very eyes. He throws the truck in park, turns off the ignition, and gets out, leaning against the door. "You may be faster, but I'm stronger. You'll get tired before I even break a sweat."

I look around. We're in the middle of nowhere. Wire livestock fencing rises from every direction and as the darkness blankets the landscape, it blends into the blackness.

Dark trees sway against the wind. Their leaves shake, sending an eerie rustling toward us on the breeze. It's not like the chase in the morning, when the sky still hung low in gray light. I could see then, at least.

I don't think Lex will hurt me—even when he gets rough in the bedroom, something holds him back—but his taut muscles ripple, making him look dangerous.

Real fucking mad.

"Ten," he begins to count. "Nine." There is a harshness in his voice that wasn't there last time.

I survey the landscape once more and take off through a field behind me. From memory, I'm trying to recall the wire fencing's location. I don't think it stands in my way in this direction.

"Eight. Seven." His countdown grows fainter as I race away.

Tall grass whips at my ankles. I take a sharp right, heading toward the trees. They beckon with their shaking leaves, inviting me to hide among the foliage and giant trunks. But it's also darker beneath their canopies.

I hear a howl. It's not an animal. No, it's Lex . . . signifying the start of the hunt.

Lex

"Ready or not, rabbit, here I come," I whisper. I take off the way she went. I calculate the moves I know she'll make. I'm not just a hunter, I'm also a tracker. Stealthy and smart.

I pick up my pace and follow her. It's so fucking dark. I don't see traces of her until they're directly in front of me.

When the tall grass sinks, ending abruptly, I know she took a right turn that shoved her heels into that very spot. What a stupid game to play. All because she called me what I am.

No, it's because of her smart-ass mouth. It's because of her defiant fucking behavior. If she wants to be a child about everything, I'll make her play hide and seek. I haven't decided what I'll do to her once I catch her. Because I will catch her. I'll make the choice the moment she's in my grasp.

Will I please her or hurt her?

A sharp pain races across my thigh, and I bite back the urge to scream out. I look down and run my hand along a barbed wire fence. A twisted point of connection is the cause of my injury. It tore a nice slit in my jeans and brought warm blood to the surface. A piece of fabric blows in the breeze, attached to another sharp piece of fencing ahead of me. I pick it off the wire and lift it to my nose. It smells like her, mixed with the metallic scent of her blood.

She's hurt.

My eyes scan the tree line, and I spot the faintest clearing of brush ahead. I run along the fence. If it connects to an adjacent paddock, I'll see it before I run into it.

"Rabbit?" I call out as I reach the cleared section. She went in there. I can feel it in my bones. My heartbeat throbs in my cock as the chase gives me a rush of adrenaline I haven't felt since I was younger.

When I became a murderer.

To be clear, I didn't get hard from the killings, but they released all these good hormones that made me wonder why more people didn't kill those they hated. It's the ultimate release. Like an orgasm for my brain. I'm hard now because my body anticipates the moment I'll get my hands on her.

As I barrel through the brush, I knock back branches

and make my way through the dark, silent forest. The old me burns beneath my skin. Dark thoughts creep from the deepest recesses of my mind to argue with me. Images of what I'll do once I catch her swirl through my thoughts.

I want to fuck her one last time.

Lexington tells me that our backs are against the wall. I have to get rid of her because she'll never just leave. My thoughts weave through the evil ones. It would be better for her if I just . . . ended it. Quick and painless. For her, not for me. It will gut me and fracture the illusion of happiness I've had since I met her. Well, since I took her.

But can I do it?

I'll figure that out once I catch her.

Branches rustle. It's disorienting and difficult to tell which direction the sound came from. I leave it up to my instinct, which drags me to the left. In the following silence, I wonder if the sound was just an animal after all. Maybe even a real rabbit. But it happens again, louder and closer, with footfalls behind it. It's a rabbit, alright.

Mine.

The toe of my shoe catches beneath a root and sends me forward, my palms landing on a rock. Her footsteps will be quieter on the rocks than on the forest floor littered with brittle twigs and dried leaves. I smirk and look up. The wall of stone nearly blends with the darkness.

"Very wise, little rabbit," I call to the top. As I climb, I realize her smaller stature has given her the advantage here.

Prey 1, Predator 0.

I slide down the rock, scraping my hands into a bloody mess on my way down. "Fuck," I growl.

I follow the wall of rocks, trying to find an easier way up. Just as I expect, there's a trail of mud and pine needles that, as steep as it is, is cake in comparison. I know that sneaky little rabbit is up there, hiding and hoping I don't find her.

Or maybe she hopes I will.

If so, that's not very wise on her part because I have no idea whether I'll devour her, kill her, or release her unscathed.

Ignoring the pain in my hands and the blood dripping down my leg, I reach the top and scan the new landscape. It's less dense than the forest floor, lacking massive trees on all sides of me. A scraping sound draws my attention to the lower rock wall. Selena slides down the last bit of scree and hops to the forest floor once more.

Sneaky fucking rabbit.

Prey 2, Predator 0.

I'm proud of her because she's showing her true wit and strength. She isn't just a *compliant* woman. She isn't just a prim and proper girl in a fancy fucking car. She's keen and willful. She's someone who can get dirty and outrun me. She doesn't seem so weak and vulnerable now. Prey can't survive by being weak. They survive on their cunning.

I dig my fingers into my waistband. As frustrated as I am, I make my way back down the cliff, sliding every few steps along the muddy path. I follow her footprints, neither of us running any longer. We depend on our wits, not speed.

Our tact.

Our instinct.

Her footprints stop, as if she vanished into thin air. As if I had imagined her from the start. I look around, letting my eyes adjust to the new layout.

Where are you, rabbit?

My eyes drop to the tree trunks lining a section of the path. I put my foot against one on the left, the other on the right, and hand over hand, tree over tree, make it to the other side where her footprints resume.

She's fucking resourceful, I'll give her that.

Prey 3, Predator o.

I nearly call it off, ending the hunt as a predator with an empty belly. But then I see her. She's perched low behind brush, looking in the direction she thinks I'll come from. She probably didn't expect me to continue this way when her footprints vanished. She underestimates me as much as I underestimated her.

My breath quickens, and my heartbeat thunders. Drool forms beneath my tongue. I creep up behind her, every meticulous step avoiding the twigs beneath my feet. Like a jaguar, I skulk among the shadows to sneak up on my next meal.

And I pounce.

I catch her and don't bother to cover her mouth as I knock her onto her back and fight her flailing arms and legs. There's no one to hear the sounds she'll make, so I let her scream. With her body sinking into the mud, I still haven't decided what I'll do with her. Lexington wants to play, and the dark part of me fights the temptation to do more than fuck her. The haunting sounds of my past whisper in my ears. I growl.

"Fuck you, Lex!" she yells as she strains against my grasp on her wrists.

"Sneaky fucking rabbit."

She whimpers as I turn her onto her stomach. I tug down her leggings, exposing her pale ass and thighs.

I unzip my jeans and rip open the button. "Nothing has changed, but I'm going to fuck you how I want one last time because I won your body, fair and square."

"I don't want you to fuck me if it's going to be the last," she says.

I laugh. "After all that, rabbit? I'm going to fuck you. The predator doesn't catch the prey to let it go. Not a good predator, at least."

I pull her hips up, spit in my hand, and rub it along my cock before pushing inside her. She gasps as I fuck her in the rough, hellish way I want, with every thrust forcing my frustration and anger through her. I push the thrill of the hunt inside her, relentlessly fucking her as if every moment she outsmarted me deserves a moment where Lexington—the man I hide from her, even as she whispers his name—can come out and play.

"Lex," she whimpers, turning her head to the side, and I don't know what she wants. I can't care at this moment.

I can't.

I answer her by fisting her hair with a hand coated in blood and mud. When I crane her neck, I go deeper than she can take. I fuck her like her pussy is mine, even while knowing I have to give it back. Her body tenses with the fear I've caused her. *Me.* Not the men I worried would hurt her. Instead, I'm the one hurting her—emotionally and physically.

Which is worse than the men who would just break her body.

A tear rolls down her cheek, and I fight the urge to wipe it away. My hips drive her into the soft ground, and I try to ignore the parts of her that will force back the side of me I *need* to feel to let her go. I ignore the soft waves of her dark hair, sticky with sweat, blood, and dirt. I force my gaze above her head instead of at her clenched eyes. Instead of the whimper of pain that leaves her lips with every thrust, I focus on the leaves rustling around us.

The world goes silent, and a nauseating echo of whimpers projects around me. I can't continue to ignore those sounds in this eerie silence. Lexington can't stand to hear them, either.

I stop thrusting and rest my pelvis against her ass. Even when she isn't so willing, she's warm and inviting. She never cries or begs for me to stop, and I can't help but find respect within her anguish and stoic fear.

My cock twitches inside her, and I want to keep going, but the need to comfort her overcomes that primal urge to feast on my last meal.

"Goddamn it." With a deflated breath, I release her hair. I'm disappointed with myself for the inability to do what I need to do to make her hate me so she'll run.

I pull out of her and turn her onto her back. My hand rubs along her torn shirt, blood drying along a huge gash in her abdomen. Mud spreads over her pale torso. Fear and tears gloss her eyes, but she doesn't tense as I lean over her. I lift her thighs and pull her against me. She's slick with mud, and I paint my handprints along her inner thighs as I spread her and push myself back inside. No matter how scared she may have been, she's still warm and wet for me.

She gasps and digs her fingers into the soft ground. I drive my hips into hers, as deep as I can. She's the only thing in my life that feels right. Safe.

And she can't be.

"I can't keep fighting you on this, Selena," I whisper. The moment I look her in the eyes, I weaken. "I'm sorry I got rough with you, but it doesn't change anything." I lean down and bite the side of her neck. I curl my hips into her and make love to her because I know it's the last time I'll be inside her. I wrap my hand around the back of her neck and bury my face into her as I thrust. "I want you to forget me after tonight."

"No, Lex." She lifts her chest. "I can't forget you. I'll remember you whenever my hands touch cool mud. I'll think of you when the leaves crunch beneath my feet. Whenever I run, I'll always imagine you're behind me."

I sit up and meet her gaze. "Rabbit, don't say that to me." As much as I want to live in her mind forever, I need for her to let me go. The nagging voice in my head returns, threatening her life, telling me that letting her live will hurt her worse. "What can I do to get *you* to let *me* go? How can I make you forget me?"

"You'd have to kill me," she says. The sickeningly calm way she says it sounds like me.

And that makes me feel worse.

I wrap my hand around the front of her throat and squeeze. She doesn't even fight me as her abdomen draws in and her body begs for a breath. She just accepts it. Whatever all this is to her, it's somehow worth dying for.

If I keep my grip on her throat just a few seconds longer, the conflict inside me will die with her. My resolve is weakening, though.

I release her neck, and she pants for air.

"I said I'd do anything for you, but I can't do the one thing I need to do," I whisper. I give her a forceful thrust to draw her full attention to me. "Promise me one thing?"

She nods before she even hears my request.

"If we get caught before we reach the border, tell the police I abducted you. Tell them I abused you, forced my way inside you, and threatened to kill you. Say anything you have to against my name to preserve yours. If the police come and shit hits the fan, don't be the wolf. Be the scared little rabbit and run."

She shakes her head.

"Promise me, rabbit. I'm not playing around with you. You still have a chance at freedom. I don't."

She looks up at me, her eyes rounding with sadness. She pulls me into her and kisses me. "I promise," she whispers.

That's all it takes to silence Lexington and the altruistic way I want to save her from me or any other person who can hurt her.

The chase. The hunt. The catch. Her promise.

Maybe she's precisely where she needs to be: a place where her demons can play freely with mine. Under the watchful eye of the wolf, the rabbit will live another day.

Chapter Eighteen

Selena

O ur little game delays our departure. By the time we get back inside, I'm a bloody, muddy mess with an ache between my legs. Lex stopped holding back and fucked me so hard and raw. I felt his strength with every deep thrust that rearranged my insides. When he choked me, I felt what he was capable of. He could kill me, and I truly thought for a few moments that he would, that I would die beneath Lex while his cock was buried inside me. For some reason, that didn't seem as bad as it should have. I still don't know if he'll let me stay with him. He told me I won, but I fear he'll change his mind.

While I shower, he moves the piece of shit's body off the porch. I run my hand over the large cut on my abdomen and rub away the dirt. I wash my hair and get rid of the twigs and leaves tangled within.

When I get out of the shower, Lex stares at me. He's still filthy, caked in dried mud and blood, and I have no clue if it's mine, his, or the man's. He gestures to the folded pile of clothes he set on the counter. Without speaking, he strips naked, and I try to look away as he pushes past me, rubbing against my body as he gets in the shower. I dress to the wordless sound of his shower. The tight feeling in my belly proves I still don't believe him. I still fear he only said what he said because he was inside me.

I grab my bag and the homeowner's key to the old Ford pickup before walking down the long driveway toward where Lex left the car before our game. When I get to the rusty tan truck, I notice Lex left the window open. The ripped driver's seat is wet from a quick rain that just passed. I groan and climb inside to back the truck toward the house.

While Lex showers, I load the truck with food and tools. I grab a hunting rifle and a box of ammo off the mantle above the fireplace and a cozy blanket from the couch. I put them in the bed of the truck. Just as I finish, Lex appears, clean and dressed. His dirty-blond hair is brushed back, still slick and wet. He surveys what I've done with a look of pride.

Actually, I'm not sure if he's proud or just less angry than he was when he first told me I wasn't going with him.

Before I can tell Lex the seat is wet, he gets into the driver's side. He slams his hand on the steering wheel. He's so on edge.

"You left the window open," I say as I get into the dry passenger seat. "Also, I put a sign on the front door saying he was out of town the rest of the week."

Lex turns toward me and nods. "Good idea."

I reach into the glove box and grab the rabbit's foot I took from my old car and hang it on the crooked rearview mirror. The corners of Lex's mouth creep upward, but he sobers. It's been our lucky charm so far, and I sure as hell wouldn't leave it behind now. It swings with the rough movements of the old truck as we pull down the driveway.

"Lex," I say, trying to draw his attention.

His lips tighten, forcing back any response. The silence makes me almost certain he said what he said to get me on the road with him. To shut me up and get me in the car so he can do what he always intended to do: drop me off the first chance he gets.

I don't truly settle in my seat until we drive by the sign for a bus station. I release a breath of relief as we pass it.

I'm confused as much as it seems he is. How can he like to be around me when he's so willing to kill me in the same moment? I try to shake off my insecurity. He was always willing to kill me. It's always been on the table, even when I felt the hesitation every time he threatened it. Even when I worried he'd do it, I knew there was a bigger struggle inside him. So I stayed calm, placing my fate in his hands.

Whatever that would be.

I'd rather him kill me than drop me off at the damn bus station. He's the first person who's gotten to know me. Not even my parents let me open up the way I have with him. They thought I had nothing more going for me than being an unhappy wife in a marriage I never wanted. But Lex saw something else in me. Something I couldn't even see. Lex is someone I should stay far away from, but I see things in him he can't either.

His darkness deserves some light.

"You surprised me, rabbit," he says after a nauseating length of silence.

"When?"

"In the woods. You were so tactful. Resourceful. Almost more than me." He lets a smirk cross his face for a moment.

"I'm not as stupid or weak as you think I am," I tell him while forcing my gaze out the window.

"I never thought you were weak." He takes a moment to gather his thoughts. "I considered you vulnerable."

"And?"

He clears his throat. "My trip to the border is suicide." He refuses to look at me as my gaze snaps to his face.

"What do you mean?"

"My story either ends in a shootout at the checkpoint or I die in the goddamn desert trying to cross on foot."

"Lex," I whisper, shaking my head.

"This is why I needed you to go. I needed you to leave because I realized what a fucking pipe dream this was. You think this is your fairy tale, but it's merely a horror story."

"I'm not accepting that."

Lex laughs. "Sure are stubborn, aren't you? You can't buy your way out of this one, rabbit." He doesn't speak for a while, letting the road noise fill the gap in our conversation. "What was your idea? How did you see this ending?" he finally asks.

"Nope, it doesn't matter."

"Rabbit," he says firmly. "Tell me."

I don't respond, dropping my head to my hand. Lex pulls over and fists my hair, pulling me into him. "Tell me, sweet bunny," he whispers. His words are the heat that melts me and he knows it does. He flashes those blue eyes at me, and my resolve dissolves.

"Fine. We used to have a nanny—"

Lex rolls his eyes.

"You know what? Forget it."

"I'm sorry," he says with a sarcastic tone. "Please, continue. You had a nanny . . ."

"I'm not going to help you if you're going to make fun of

how I grew up. Would you like it if I made fun of how you grew up?"

"You're right. I had a nanny, though, for your information. He was the local drug dealer."

I curl my lip. "Anyway, my nanny was from Arkansas, and she always talked about this forest, saying you could get lost in there and no one would ever find you. Wichita? Or something?"

"Ouachita. It's a national forest," he corrects me. When I cock my head at him, he shrugs. "A lot of time to study when you're serving life."

"Yeah, Ouachita. She said people built cabins there and just lived off the grid."

"What's the point of this little tale?"

"The point is, maybe we can find someplace down there to hide out instead of trying to cross the border."

Lex releases my hair and sits back. "That's not . . . a bad idea," he says, as if formulating a new plan in his mind.

We take the exit toward Arkansas. We'd have gone through there anyway, but now we'll make a little pit stop, because what else do we have to lose?

WE DRIVE into Ouachita National Park through a utility road entrance, avoiding the front gate. A sign attached to a robust tree trunk warns us to enter the heart of the forest at our own risk. We're fine with the risk.

The narrow trail pulls us into the depths of the park. Dense trees surround us in ways I've never seen. It's so thick. So lush. So green. Aside from the path, this place has been completely left to nature and even then, the truck bounces as we drive over large tree roots trying to reclaim that, too. We take another unmarked road, driving further through winding woodlands. Then we take another—and another—until we have no idea where we are, which means no one else will know, either.

Lex yawns, which makes me yawn. He cuts off the engine.

"Let's get in the back of the truck," he says as he climbs out. He unlocks the gate, climbs inside, and goes right to loading up the rifle with rounds.

I get out of the truck, and my feet land on the soft forest floor. When I close the door, the warm, humid night air wraps around me. The forest roars with nighttime sounds: big insects chirping, mosquitoes buzzing, and trees creaking. I climb into the back and close the tailgate.

Lex lays out the blanket I brought, covering the dirty metal. He pulls another blanket from a bag. He lies down and puts the bag beside him so I can lay my head on it. I lie beside him, and it reminds me of the overlook, when I found myself snuggling a man I shouldn't.

I still shouldn't, but now I need to.

Lex wraps his arms around me, and I lay my head on his chest. The faint smell of soap still clings to his skin. He covers me and rests his head on his other arm.

"It's peaceful here," I whisper.

"I haven't figured out if it's a good idea yet."

"It seems like a good idea for tonight, at least."

I lean up and kiss him. He grabs my chin and tugs me away from his mouth. "Not tonight," he says. He's still on edge.

"What's wrong?" I ask.

"I feel like I have to protect you. We're in the middle of

a forest I'm not familiar with, so I have to pay attention to the shit around us," he says as he releases my chin.

"There's nothing around us, Lex. Relax."

He shakes his head. "That's what you don't understand. I haven't dropped my guard since I got in your car that night. Even before I slept with you, I kept my eyes open for the police, your husband, or anyone that could hurt you. You wanted to stay with me, and I let you stay. Now I have to be more vigilant than ever."

I rub my hand down his stomach, inching toward the front of his jeans. He grabs my hand and rubs my palm.

"I said no," he tells me, so firmly that I nearly listen.

I shrink beneath the blanket and work off the button until his pawing protests grow weak.

"Don't do what you're thinking, Selena," he whispers through a frustrated groan. "You know once you put your mouth on me, I'm done."

"That's the point," I say before kissing the warm skin above his pants. I work his jeans open, pull out his cock, and take him into my mouth.

"Naughty fucking rabbit," he growls and takes the blanket off so he can see me. He winds his hand through my hair and groans as I bob on him, taking him as far into my mouth as I can, letting him raise his hips to make me take that last inch. When I pull away and look up at him, I wipe the drool from my lower lip.

"Put your mouth back on me, bunny," he whispers as he pushes my head down.

I love pleasing him. I love the way he melts from my touch, causing him to say my nickname again, so endearing and so seductive. I can't believe I once hated it. I'll be anything he wants me to be when he calls me that now.

Lex wraps his hand around my throat, pulling me

toward his mouth and kissing me, hard and driven. I moan against his lips.

"Fuck. Your mouth is incredible. Let me devour you." He pulls away and holds his pants up as he unlocks the tailgate and drags me toward the edge.

I sit up and let my legs dangle over the side. Lex kisses me before removing my shoes and jeans. He lays me back, wraps his arms around my pale thighs, and tugs me toward him. Just like he said he would, he leans down and devours me, licking me in long strokes that make me grip the blanket above my head. I moan as he rakes my inner thighs with rough fingertips.

"Your pussy is like something I've never tasted, bunny, and I could eat you all fucking night," he groans as he strokes himself and licks me. His tongue dips inside me before slowly curling over my clit.

"Lexington," I moan.

He sits up and growls with a sadistic smirk before pushing three fingers inside me. He doesn't even try to work me out, and I whimper.

"Get on your hands and knees."

I swallow before doing as he says. The metal scrapes my knees as I back toward him. I'm vulnerable and open, and my cheeks flush with embarrassment.

Lex bites my inner thighs and makes his way up to my pussy again. He buries his face into me, looping his hands around my legs to keep me from moving away from him. The tips of his fingers burn my hips as he squeezes and draws me closer. I moan and drop my chest. His tongue moves at a whole new angle, running along the hood of my clit instead of against it. He moves his head from side to side, and I tremble.

"Come on my face so I can fuck you while you're still

spasming." His warm breath washes over my clit and when he starts moving his tongue again, it makes me shudder. He loves how he makes me feel.

And I love it, too.

The sounds of the forest die, and I hear nothing more than the sloppy sounds of him fucking me with his mouth. I hear the hungry groan between each stroke of his tongue.

"Have you ever squirted?" he asks.

"No," I whimper.

Lex pulls me by my hips, drawing me off the back of the truck. I feel empty without his tongue on me. He bends me over the open tailgate and kicks my legs open. He stands beside me with his body pressed against mine. His hand caresses my ass before his fingers push inside me, stretching me with three fingers as he uses the full strength of his arm. He's so fast. So hard. And I feel the intense urge to bear down on his fingers. I scream out as it grows too intense, vibrating my entire body.

"Lex!" I call out. I don't know what I'm feeling, and I'm not sure I like it.

"Shh, bunny, relax and let it happen," he whispers over the intensifying sounds of wetness between my legs. When I tense, he pulls his fingers out of me, and a quick emptiness follows with a gush of liquid.

Before I can say anything, before I even know if I like it, his fingers are back inside me, fucking me with a hungry strength that tenses my body all over again. When he pulls out, I shudder and come again in a wave of pleasure.

"It's too intense," I say as I reach back and touch his thigh.

"Come like that on my cock, and I'll stop," he says with a smirk.

I nod, and he gets behind me. My chest presses against

the open tailgate as he leans his weight into me, gripping the back of my neck with a frustrated groan. He pushes inside me, slick and wet with my come. He fucks me hard and fast, with the same rough momentum that made me saturate the ground with my come. The angle is just right, and every thrust makes my body tremble in noticeable waves. When the pressure becomes too much, he pulls out and keeps his cock against my pussy as I cover him in a gush of come. He grips my ass as I drip around the length of his dick still pressed against my swollen clit.

"Such a good girl," he growls as he strokes himself against me, stroking my clit at the same time. "Messy little bunny. You're fucking soaked." He pushes himself back inside me.

My body tenses as he fucks me, and I realize it's from my body wanting more. More of him. Not just his body, but his heart.

"Do you have feelings for me, Lex?" I ask, and it stops him mid-thrust.

"What a time to ask me that," he says as he leans over me. "If I said no, would you want me to stop fucking you?"

I tense, and he groans as I tighten around him.

Couldn't he just fucking lie while he's inside me? Does he have to be so . . . cold?

"Oh, that made you mad, huh? You can't imagine that I didn't get feelings like you did after all our experiences and time together?"

My heart. I feel the cracks run through it, and I fight back tears. If I speak, he'll know he's upsetting me.

Lex wraps an arm around my chest and lifts me to his. He bites my neck. "Bunny, you have all that's left of my heart. Anything I *can* feel is for you."

Just like that, his words crawl through the cracks in my heart and seal them. I melt into his strong body.

"I don't know if I know what love is, Selena, but I know this is the closest I've felt to another person." He pulls out of me and turns me to face him. He draws me close to his mouth. "I wanted you to leave because I needed to protect the one person who made me feel *something* other than numb or angry. The only person capable of humanizing someone as barbaric as me."

I swallow, his breath mixing with mine. "I don't know what love is either, Lex. I never have. I just know it wasn't what I had with my husband, and that's why I didn't want to leave you. Leaving meant losing the one thing that made me feel . . . safe." The word almost catches in my throat, but I manage to get it out.

Lex buttons his jeans, climbs into the truck bed, and motions to me. I dress and climb up with him. We lie down, and he holds me tight. I feel bad he didn't finish, especially when he made me come the way he did. I slip my hand down his stomach, but he stops me with a firm grip.

"We'll play more once we find a cabin. And I'll give you twice the amount of my come."

I nod and kiss him before rolling onto my back and staring up at the dark, star-filled sky. I've never seen something so beautiful. So peaceful. It feels like home, and I'm surprised how little I miss my family and my old life.

But what can my new life possibly be?

Chapter Nineteen

Lex

There it is. A quaint cabin tucked away in the middle of the national park, far away from everyone and everything. The whole outside is natural wood, aging ungracefully. Big solar panels line the moss-covered roof. At least there's electricity, which is more than I expected. Selena cranes her head to see what I see.

It's perfect.

We leave the truck a little ways back and follow an over-grown path on foot. She keeps looking at me as we walk, and I know she wants to know why I stopped us from fucking more last night. Her brain is probably in overdrive, trying to figure out what she did wrong. She didn't do anything wrong. It's all in my head. Even then, I still did what I needed to do to make her come, because that's what matters.

There's no way to explain to her what I felt. In that moment, I realized just how important she was to me. You'd think realizing that would have made me want to keep going. Fuck her better. But the foreign, uncomfortable feeling did the opposite. It made me close up.

I knew what to do with her pussy but not her heart.

I'll make it up to her. I'll make her forget I ever stopped us last night.

"What do we do if someone is home?" I ask, trying to get out of my head because it's not a place I like to stay in.

"Get rid of them," she says without looking away from the cabin in front of us.

There she goes, surprising me again with how dark and dangerous she's become.

"Sadistic fucking rabbit," I say through gritted teeth. I feel guilty that she has no qualms about killing someone else. Decades of coldness froze me. She may have warmed me, but she's also taking my coldness as her own. Now I'm freezing her. Even thawed, I have no issue killing, and that's how I know just how fucked I am. But she doesn't deserve this.

We stop just outside the yard behind some trees and bushes. We watch and wait, but there aren't signs of anyone having been there in a while. Weeds grow upward and have overtaken a wheelbarrow leaned against the wall of a shed. Its tire has been reduced to a pile of melted rubber beneath it. Tattered curtains line some of the windows, which are dirty and broken in some places.

We head toward the front door, looking over our shoulders. I rub my hand along the rickety wooden door. Humidity has warped its edges. I grab the doorknob, and it turns with a rattle because of a missing screw. The moment I open the door, I smell it. I recognize the scent as if I'm thrown back into my childhood within one breath.

"What's that smell?" she asks as she covers her nose with her hand.

"That, rabbit, is the smell of death."

Her eyes widen. "What do you mean?"

I motion for her to wait here. I don't need to worry about protecting us both, but that smell makes me fairly certain I know what's home, and it's not someone living. "Just stay here for a minute," I tell her as I load a round in the rifle.

The smell intensifies as I walk toward the back of the cabin. When I turn the corner, I see a man in a recliner. He's slumped over, the television's remote still in his mottled hand. His face is gray, but he hasn't been dead all that long.

I'm so used to the smell that I hardly notice it at all. I'm almost completely nose blind to the familiarity. "Well, that's fucking convenient," I say through a laugh.

I can't help but think the luck is from her stupid little rabbit's foot, which is nestled in my pocket.

I go back to the front door and find Selena still covering her nose. "Can't kill what's already dead," I tell her.

"What?" she asks, breathing through her mouth.

"Whoever owns this place is very dead in their room." I start to open the windows, struggling against the years of grime to pry them open.

"We can't stay here. It smells like death. Literally."

I stop and stare at her. What does she mean we can't *stay* here? It's everything we've been searching for. It's more than what we could ever ask for, smell or no smell. "We couldn't be any luckier, and you want to leave because of a little smell?"

"It's not little."

"Once I get the body out, the smell will go away. Mostly."

"I'll wait out here," she says as she waves me off and goes to a wicker rocking chair on the porch.

I enter the room and glance at the sad sap before trying to figure out how best to get rid of him. My fingers are crossed as I head into the backyard through an even rick-etier backdoor to check the shed. A dingy blue tarp catches my eye, and I yank it out, knocking over a shovel and rake as it comes free. When I head back inside, I lay out the tarp on the floor in front of him.

"Sorry, buddy," I tell him as I shove him off the chair. I haven't apologized to men I've killed before, but here I am, apologizing to a long-dead corpse. Selena's warmth has thawed me a bit more than I'm willing to admit.

The man hits the tarp with a thud that sounds like a garbage bag filled with congealed pudding and bones. The skin on his left arm has begun to slough away, revealing the sinewy highway beneath. I almost laugh when I realize how much this doesn't disgust me. Not even the dark stain of human decay left behind on the chair elicits more than a shrug of my shoulders.

I wrap up the tarp, tie it off with rope, and drag him out the back door. I walk as far into the woods as I can and leave him there—in the humid heat but out of the sun, at least. I'll come back and bury him later, after I've dealt with the chair.

When I go back inside, it's already smelling better. I grab a half-smoked cigar off the table beside the chair and light it with the old Zippo resting beside it. My cheeks puff at the rich smoke, a strong scent that somehow overpowers the perfume of death. It feels good to have it between my lips. I miss the normalcy of having a smoke.

A legal one, at least.

The recliner is light enough to lift. The fabric smells

like old man, piss, and death. Definitely not up to Selena's standards. I carry it outside, letting the cigar mask the scent as I go. I lean it against the back of the shed, which is about all I'm willing to do with it in the stifling heat.

I circle to the front of the house and wipe my hands on my pants as I lean against the railing surrounding the front porch. The doors are wide open to let the stench clear, and flies and other insects buzz in and out.

Selena's eyes roll up and stop at the cigar. "Since when do you smoke?"

I smirk, drawing the cigar from my lips. "Since I was eight."

"Jesus," she says with a shake of her head.

I offer it to her. "Want to try?"

She chews the inside of her cheeks before taking it and putting it between her full lips. If she knew it was half-smoked by the dead man himself, she wouldn't have taken it. She puffs on it and hands it back.

"Since when do *you* smoke?" I ask, a sly smile on my face. From the way her lips wrapped around it, I have the feeling it isn't her first time.

She shrugs. "On and off since I was eighteen. Mostly off. How'd you know?"

I step toward her, lift her chin, and look down at her. "Because you smoke like you've done it before. And it's fucking sexy." I run my thumb along her lower lip.

Her eyes roll back at my touch but then she rips her face away and wipes at her mouth. "Dude, you were just disposing of a dead body."

I let the cigar rest between my lips. I smirk at her and go inside to wash my hands. If she only knew about all the things we touched in prison, and honestly, most were worse than a dead guy.

Coffee mugs and a single plate fill one side of the sink. I wash my hands, turning the knob and realizing there's no hot water. I'm not sure how Selena will feel about this. Actually, I do know. She's going to hate it. But she'll deal with it for me. Which I hate. I still haven't told her the shower is merely a stall outside with a hose attached to a rusty showerhead.

When I turn around, she's behind me, sneaky little prey. At least her hand isn't pressed against her nose any longer, which means the smell is getting better. Or she is getting used to it. Regardless, she still has a scowl on her face. I can't help but chuckle.

"Not good enough for you?" I ask.

"It's just so . . ."

"It's all we have, rabbit. What'd you think would be out here? The Ritz Carlton?"

She blows hair from her forehead. "I know. I know."

"You still have a chance to back out. I can still take you to the bus station."

Her eyes narrow. "No."

"Then enjoy what you won in our little game of hide and seek. You got to stay with me, just like you wanted." I'm struggling to find sympathy for her. While this place is a downgrade for her, it's an upgrade for me.

I turn around and start washing the dishes. Maybe she'll feel better without the memory of a person's dirty life strewn in front of her. My hands redden from the chill of the water.

"Hey, at least he didn't die in the bed," I call to her as she sneaks a peek around the corner. You get used to finding silver linings when everything else in your life is just a different shade of gray.

"I'm not sleeping in there," she says. She strolls through

the living room and prods the red couch, ignoring the lumps in the cushions. She pushes her weight down on the springs and rips away the cushions.

I turn around, dry my hands on a towel, and lean back against the sink.

"It's a pull-out couch," she says with a beaming smile that tugs at my lips, too.

"Do they even have those where you came from?"

She drops the old frame and snaps her gaze to me. I raise my hands. I don't know why she gets so mad when I give her shit about being rich. I don't care when she says things about me being poor. It's just what we are and where we differ.

I walk over to her and wipe the sweaty hair from her cheek before nudging her aside and releasing the rickety pull-out. The lumpy mattress is stained with signs of age, but it looks clean enough for a fancy show rabbit.

"I hope the quarters are to your liking, your majesty," I say with a playful bow. She doesn't find the humor in it. I'm not sure what's on her mind, but it's making her pissy.

I lie on the bed and tug her into me. The old mattress coils whine, and Selena lets out a squeal. I guess now is the time to confront the big elephant in the room.

"What's the matter, rabbit? You've been weird since last night."

When she doesn't answer, I roll over her and spread her legs with my knees. I look down at her trembling lower lip. If she's not upset about my denial last night, I'm not sure what it's about. She's probably full of regret for staying with me in this decrepit cabin that still smells like a dead man.

"You can leave, Selena. No one is forcing you to stay here."

She fights back the gloss in her eyes.

"What do you want?" I ask louder and shake her shoulders.

"You wouldn't understand," she says, shaking her head.

She always thinks I don't understand. I understand more than she realizes. "Why? Why the fuck wouldn't I understand? I wasn't born with a golden fucking spoon in my mouth, but I can still understand you."

Her eyes widen. "Fuck you, Lex," she says through a huff and tries to squeeze out from beneath me.

"So goddamn mouthy for such a little thing."

My words strike her harder than any fists could. I can only imagine the things her husband used to say that made her close herself off so tightly and lock her heart away. Until a criminal like me came along and knew how to pick it open.

She flails beneath me, but I pin her wrists and lean over her. "Tell me what's bothering you, rabbit." I lower my voice the way she likes. "Talk to me."

She blinks and finally releases the tears she's been holding back. "I . . . I just . . . I don't want you to be so okay with me leaving. You keep asking me to leave. Telling me to leave. You're pushing me away!" Her voice fills with anger instead of sadness.

"You really think I fucking *want* you to leave?"

She lifts her chin, drumming up confidence from some-where inside her. "Yeah, I do."

"For once in my goddamn life I was being selfless and thinking about the wellbeing of someone else. I didn't *want* you to leave. I *needed* you to leave because it was safer for you." I lift my gaze to the wall, staring at a rosary hanging from a hook. I drop my eyes to her once more. "I've never felt guilt. I was born like this. Something not quite right in the head. But I knew if you got in trouble for all this, or killed, I would *never* get past that."

"Let me decide what I'm willing to risk."

"I wanted to let you go so you'd be safe at home. I could imagine a life with you I could never have. I could think about how happy you made me when I've always thought I was incapable of such a *normal* emotion. The only thing that ever made me happier than you was fucking killing. And the part of me that enjoys hurting people? I didn't want him to hurt you, either."

"You wouldn't hurt me," she says with a shake of her head.

I choke back a laugh. "I could. And I almost did, more times than you know. I've been willing to kill you since the day I took you."

"I don't believe that, Lex." The shake of her head intensifies, as if reasoning with herself more than me.

"I pushed you away so you could be with someone *better*. I wanted you to have better than the small life I could ever give you. This? This rundown cabin? It's what I can give you." I inhale a sharp breath. It's not good enough for her, I know that. She knows that. We both do. "People describe love as not being able to be away from that person, that it's such a horrible thing to be apart, but it didn't feel like I loved you when I selfishly wanted to keep you for myself. I may not know what love feels like, but I knew enough to know that loving you meant letting you go." I fight back the heat behind my eyes, which I don't remember ever feeling in my entire life. "Old me would have kept you, fucked you, and killed you when I was done with you. New me, the one you drew out, wanted you to forget me and live the life you deserved."

"Even now, you want me to leave," she whispers, her voice wavering with the tremble of her body.

"Because you look so fucking unhappy," I say as I cut my gaze.

"I'm unhappy because you make me feel unwanted."

I sit back and pull her onto my lap. "I've wanted you since the moment I saw you in that car. I've never not wanted you."

She drops her head to my shoulder, and I hear the breathy sounds of her trying not to cry as I hold her.

"If I wasn't in this situation, bunny, I would never let you go or push you away."

She flashes her eyes up at me. "I'm a killer, too, Lex."

I shake my head. "You wouldn't be if it weren't for me."

"This isn't just *your* situation anymore. It's *ours*. Stop thinking of me as the girl you dragged to hell and realize that maybe I've already been there."

"Fuck, bunny." I grip the back of her neck and kiss her. "If you want this, I'll give you everything I can in this little world of ours." I pull away and touch her cheek with a warm palm.

Chapter Twenty

Selena

We've been living our new life for a few nights now, and it quickly became clear we'd need more money, even while living off-grid. Much like the guy who lived in this cabin before us, Lex has been doing odd jobs for others who have moved off the grid themselves, but it's not enough to keep food on our table. Lex keeps promising to teach me how to hunt, and I need to hold him to that one of these days.

Prey can hunt prey.

"Rabbit," Lex says as he walks in. The screen door slams behind him.

I finish drying the dish in my hand and turn to face him. "What?"

"I have an idea, but I'm not sure I can let you go with me."

"I'm going where you go."

He smirks. "I thought you'd say that. I'm going to do a little robbery. Get some quick cash."

I shake my head. "Wh-what?"

"Don't worry, rabbit, I've done jobs like this in my sleep." He walks over and brushes a dirt-covered hand across my cheek.

"You ended up in prison, Lex!"

"I was in prison for murder, not robberies."

"Who are you thinking about robbing?" I ask. We need money but committing a robbery seems like an unnecessary risk. We've committed enough felonies since the night I met Lex. On the other hand, what's one more?

"There's a small gas station down the road. No cameras. Nothing. I know they won't have much, but they'll have more than we do."

"How do you plan on doing this?"

He reaches back, pulls the pistol from his jeans, and shakes it in front of my face. "Easily." His eyes darken. "Especially with a hot little diversion."

I lift one of my eyebrows and cock my head at his statement.

"You'd be bait, little rabbit."

"They'd see our faces."

"We leave the truck, go on foot, and avoid that gas station from now on. There's plenty of others."

"Seems really fucking dumb, Lex."

"Then don't go. I don't need bait to get the job done." He tucks the pistol into his jeans again. "I'll be back later."

The moment he turns to walk away, I feel the tug at my heart. "No, I'll go."

"WHAT'S THE PLAN?" I ask as we pull onto a dead-end road about a quarter of a mile from the rustic gas station.

Lex chambers his pistol. "We separate as we get closer to the building. You draw out the clerk. I'll sneak in and take the money in the till and the safe, if there is one."

My mouth gapes. "How the hell am I going to lure the guy away from the register?"

Lex's hungry eyes rove down my body, and my cheeks flush. "You'll figure it out. You're resourceful, remember?"

We abandon the truck, and Lex pockets the keys. The sun has set, and we are ghosts walking along the dark road. Lex wraps his arm around me and drags me to the inside so he's closest to the road. What a gentleman.

The small gas station comes into view ahead. A tall black lamp post illuminates the front door. Bugs swarm around it. There's only a single pump for gas, with nozzles on both sides and enough room for two cars at any given time. This is a small and local community.

People here are way too trusting, and Lex will prey on that trusting nature. I doubt they have much more than a few dollars in the till, let alone anything worth protecting with cameras, so at least he was right about that.

Lex pushes me toward the door and walks ahead of me, looping around the building. I brush my sweaty palms on my jeans and take a deep breath before gripping the door's grimy handle. A bell rings overhead when I enter. The racks inside mostly house essentials and snacks—toothpaste, mouthwash, and deodorant alongside a variety of chips, beef jerky, and pretzels.

A door closes somewhere inside a back hallway, and footsteps draw closer. My heart races, and my eyes fall on the old desk with the even older cash register sitting on top of it. Cigarettes line the wall behind the register, waiting to be chosen beneath a worn age-restriction sign.

A balding man appears in the doorway, and he smiles when he sees me. He looks behind me. "Can I help you?"

I struggle to get out the words I need to say as guilt chokes me. I feel absolutely awful about robbing this man. He hasn't done anything to deserve a visit from us. This is where Lex and I differ. He doesn't see people as human beings. Collateral damage doesn't exist to him. There are no innocents.

"H-Hi, yes." I point toward the darkened road. "My car ran out of gas down the road."

"You walked here all by yourself?" His eyes scan me. There's a hint of suspicion in his words, and I try to pull my shit together for Lex.

"Yeah, it's not far. I'm wondering if I could buy a gallon off you." I pull some bills from my pocket and show him the money.

The man steps from behind the counter, his eyes never leaving mine. "You need a can?" he asks as he guides me toward the door.

I nod.

I follow him outside and trail behind him until we reach the circle of light from the lamp above us. I'm not going back into the darkness with him. He unlocks a door, and I can't see anything until he closes it and appears beneath the light. He's carrying an old metal gas can. "Just drop it off when you come back for more gas," he says as he hands it to me and keeps his hand outstretched for the money.

I hand him four dollars, but I catch a glimpse of Lex's shadow inside. I need to keep the man out here with me for his safety. I don't want any more death on our hands, and I'll do what I can to keep this robbery from becoming a murder. I lift the heavy jerrycan and futz with the top. As he starts to walk away, I increase the sounds of frustration leaving my lips. He finally turns back to me.

"Do you need help, miss?" he asks.

I smile and hand it back to him. He works off the cap and puts the nozzle into it. "There you go," he says, and turns to leave once more.

Fighting through panic, I reach out and graze his arm. My eyelashes flutter as I lean back against the pump. "I *really* appreciate your help, mister."

He looks at his feet, seeming bashful all of a sudden. "That's what we do here, ma'am. It's really nothing." His words make me feel fucking awful. This man will probably never trust another person in need because of me.

The meter ticks past one gallon, and I bend over to remove the nozzle from the can. Shy or not, the man is so focused on me that he doesn't notice Lex leaving. I hang the nozzle back in the pump and smile at him. "I'll bring this back," I say as I shake the can.

He nods and goes back inside. Lights turn on as he returns to the back of the store.

Lex and I hightail it back down the road. The can sloshes in my hand, and he's grinning from ear to ear. "You didn't need to steal his can," he says.

"Well, too late now."

We get to the truck, and Lex puts the can in the bed before climbing inside. The gas on my hands creates an overpowering smell when I close the cab door.

"So?" I ask once we get a little further down the road. I'm torn between hoping there wasn't much to steal from the poor guy and wanting there to be.

"I think that dude lives there. He was watching porn in a room with a rickety bed."

I curl my lip. "Gross."

"I bet he doesn't even know he's been robbed yet. Probably still finishing rubbing one out."

I fight the pang of guilt, forcing it away as I look toward Lex's pocket. "I don't care about what he was doing, Lex. What'd you get?"

"He had way more than I thought. Hardly shit in the cash register, but fat fucking stacks in his masturbation station."

"Jesus Christ," I groan. "You didn't rob him of everything he owned, did you?"

A smirk crosses his face. "Of course not, bunny. I knew that would eat at that little heart of yours. I took enough, though. Should have taken more for the way he fucked you with his eyes," he says through a growl. "You did so fucking good."

When Lex doesn't turn onto the utility road, I gesture toward it.

"We aren't going back yet. Let's go get a little something to eat at the diner. I know you like that place, and I love that no one asks fucking questions. Everyone there looks like they have a past they're running from."

Excitement swells in my gut at the thought of a hearty meal. We've been so frugal. He still hasn't told me how much he took, but I'm too distracted by the thought of good food to ask again right now.

We pull into the hole-in-the-wall diner, and Lex covers the jerrycan in the back with a blanket. "Oh, hey, I grabbed this for you," he says as he reaches into his back pocket and tosses a stick of deodorant at me.

My lips tremble. Lex cut the top layer off the cabin owner's deodorant and has been using that. I politely refused. Now I have my own to use. My heart stumbles over itself at the small but significant gesture.

I set the stick on the dashboard, but Lex shakes his head. "Nothing from the gas station in view. Put it under the seat."

I do as I'm told, and his attention to detail makes me realize why he never got caught. Well, for robberies, at least. I hope his street smarts rub off on me like the rest of him has.

Lex

THE WAITRESS ACKNOWLEDGES us with a curt nod when we head inside. Red paint peels off the seat of our chosen booth. Selena goes to get in across from me, but I grab her arm and pull her beside me.

"Hey, you two," the waitress says as she tugs out her pad of paper. "Menus?" We both shake our heads. "What can I get you?"

"A cheeseburger," Selena says with too much excitement at the thought of a greasy burger. She's nearly wiggling at the idea.

"Make it two," I tell the waitress, minus the childish excitement. "And two coffees and waters, please."

The waitress scribbles on her pad and puts it in her apron.

"It's too late for coffee," Selena says after the waitress walks away. "We'll be up all night."

"That's the plan," I say. I don't intend to sleep once we get back. And neither will she.

I look back at the empty diner. My hand rises to her throat, and she whimpers. The sound goes straight to my cock. I've been hard since we left the gas station because of how well she played her part. I lean in and kiss her, tugging at her lower lip as I bite into it. My hand moves to her thigh, and she spreads her legs for me.

"Unzip your jeans for me, bunny," I say without looking at her.

She shakes her head. "Not here."

"I want to reward you," I say, leaving no room for another objection. "Unzip those jeans and keep those thighs spread for me so I can make you come before our dinner is served. The longer you wait, the more likely it is she'll return while my fingers are still buried in your cunt."

She inhales a sharp breath, but her fingers drop to her jeans. I dip my hand beneath the splayed fabric and find her bare pussy with the tips of my fingers. Her cheeks flush the moment I run them along her wet slit. I rub her clit.

The door to the kitchen opens, and she grabs my wrist with her hand. I don't move from between her legs. She leans forward to block the view of her sweet little pussy, and the waitress smiles as she sets down two coffees and two red glasses filled with water.

"Sorry it took so long. I had to brew a new pot. Your meals will be out shortly."

"Thank you." I turn to Selena. "Didn't you want to ask for creamer, babe?" I swirl my fingers around her clit. She leans on her fist, anger radiating from her. For a show rabbit, she sure doesn't like to be shown. "Go on," I tell her.

"Can I h-have creamer?" she asks with a tremble in her voice as I dip my fingers inside her in the middle of her request.

A smirk crosses my lips as the waitress nods and grabs a

silver creamer pitcher from another table. She leaves, and Selena's eyes jump to mine. *Fuck you*, she mouths.

"Watch your mouth, rabbit, or I'll put you on your fucking knees beneath this table. See how mouthy you feel like being then."

She knows I will absolutely fuck the brattiness out of her throat, and her pelvis tilts at the thought. She loves being used, even if she doesn't want to admit it.

I keep rubbing her until she grips my thigh beneath the table. I take a casual sip of my coffee, and she struggles to keep her moans at bay beside me. She isn't getting close enough from just my touch, too panicked at the idea of getting caught.

"I want you to come, bunny. You were so *fucking* good tonight, so damn sexy. Such a good little bait rabbit. I don't know a single man that wouldn't go out of their way to help you. All you have to do is give us a look with those big, sweet eyes. Fuck," I tell her with a growl as I lower the coffee mug to the table. Her thighs tremble and her muscles tighten the more they try to close against my touch. "Come for me. Come on my fingers so I can eat my dinner with your scent still on me."

That did it for her. She grips her silverware, the metal scraping against the table as she fights the moans and the shudder of her body. A low sound slips from her and makes me ache.

The waitress returns to our table. Selena straightens her back and leans forward. I keep my hand down her pants. She sets the plates in front of us. "Let me know if you need anything else."

Selena leans back, but I don't take my hand away from the warmth of her pussy. I let the throb of her clit speak to my fingertips before I finally pull my hand away. My fingers are covered in her come, and I twitch at the sight of it. I lift my burger with both hands and bite into it. Her mouth gapes as she watches me.

"Don't look at me like that, rabbit. I told you I'm going to eat my dinner with my fingers covered in your come." I nudge her to eat, and she finally starts to devour her long-anticipated meal. Grease from the burger mixes with the sweetness of her come, and after my last bite, I put my fingers into my mouth and finally lick her off my skin.

I stare at her as she finishes eating.

I love that she's sitting in her come-soaked jeans right now, with nothing between her and the denim. She looks like she's enjoying that burger as much as she enjoyed my fingers. I wanted to give her this normalcy tonight. She deserves it. I asked her to do something very abnormal, and she did it without question. Two things, actually. I asked her to help me commit a robbery, and to come on my fingers in the middle of a diner, and she did both.

Like a good fucking girl.

The waitress comes back and puts the check on the table. When she leaves, I pull out the thick stack of money folded in my pocket and lay out two twenty-dollar bills. Selena's eyes widen. When coupled with what I make from odd jobs, the amount I took is enough to keep us going for a little while. It physically pained me to leave some of the man's money behind, but she's rubbing off on me as much as I'm rubbing off on her. I could use a little of her light. Some of her emotions.

All of her.

Chapter Twenty-One

Selena

Lex got way more money than I expected or hoped for. He wants to provide for us in a situation that hardly allows for it. He can give me a place to live, a bed where I can rest my weary head, and he can give me himself. That's all I really want, but we also *need* a little more than what the odd jobs can give. We aren't trying to be extravagant, but we must survive away from the world that will try to separate us.

Driving back from the diner has me in my feelings. I love and hate that Lex pushes me out of my comfort zone and makes me feel good. It's not just a selfless urge to make me come, though; he wants the control I hand to him at the worst times and places. He loves that I listen when everything inside me says no.

Rain begins to patter against the windshield, then the sky opens up and it starts to pour. It reminds me of the first night I met Lex. Unlike me, he's sure behind the wheel, despite the rain.

I blink heavily as my eyes try to adjust to a figure along the side of the road. Through the blur of rain on the windows, I can make out a man with his pale thumb held in the air. He has a limp, and it tears at heartstrings that should have been snipped when Lex carjacked me.

"There's a guy back there," I say, pointing behind me.

"So what?"

"We can't leave him like that."

Lex shakes his head. "We sure can, rabbit. Have you learned nothing from this whole venture? We've finally gotten our shit together so we don't have to keep running. I won't risk that because of some hitchhiker."

"But you're here with me. He's not going to do anything with you here. You're the biggest predator in these parts." I have no fear of any other man with Lex around. He'll always protect me. I push out my lower lip. "I'll feel really shitty if we leave him out there in the storm."

"Don't look at me like that. I don't like how selfless you are. I love that it put me in the car with you in the first place, but your selflessness is suicidal sometimes."

He has to remember what it was like to need a ride.

"Please," I beg. After what happened to the poor clerk, I feel like I need to make amends to the universe and improve one person's day to account for robbing the gas station.

"Jesus fucking Christ, Selena, fine. But so help me God, if he even thinks about touching you, you're going to wish I never stopped to pick him up. His death will be on your hands."

He slams on the brakes, throws the truck in reverse, and backs toward the man. At first I think I must have imagined him because he seems to have vanished within the darkness, but a knock on the window startles me and throws me right back into the night I met Lex. It feels like déjà vu.

Lex lowers my window a little and speaks over me. "Do you need help?" I'm sure the man can tell how much he doesn't want to ask. He couldn't seem less approachable if he tried.

The man stares at us. Rain plasters his dark hair to his forehead. He looks young, closer to my age, and he's not nearly as intimidating as Lex. "Depends. What kind of help are you offering?"

The rain finds its way through the cracked window and wets my jeans. At least it kind of hides the fact that I came just a little while ago and soaked my pants.

Lex seems annoyed by his evasive response. "A ride or a place to stay for the night."

The man looks ahead at the dark, dreary, wet road. "I could use a place to stay for the night, if it's not too much trouble."

"Hop in," Lex says with an annoyed sigh.

I move over, sidling up to Lex so the man can get in. He has that same smell Lex had—a heavy, earthy aroma that sticks with you long after you dry.

"I'm Jamie," the man says. His wet clothes soak into mine.

"I'm Ben, and this is my wife," Lex says.

"Does she have a name?" Jamie asks.

"It doesn't matter what her name is. She's my wife and that's all you need to know."

Lex is being rude. The guy is only trying to introduce himself to us. He seems innocent enough. I know Lex is mistrustful, and I understand why, but nothing and no one will separate us now. I'm confident of that.

The rest of the drive back to the cabin is heavy and silent, and I fight back my urge to ask why he was walking along the road. The longer he's in the car with us, the more I worry I've made the wrong choice. We worked so hard to find a place where we didn't have to run anymore, and now I'm putting us at risk because of residual guilt from the robbery.

We pull onto the utility road and take the winding path to the cabin. We get out of the truck once we park in the spot where the tires sink into the familiar section of ground. Lex gets out first and opens the passenger door. His lips draw tightly downward as the rain begins to soak his clothing. The man beside me scoots out of the truck and Lex steps aside so he can get down.

"You live out here?" he asks.

"The fewer questions you ask, the better," Lex says.

We walk into the cabin, and the heaviness continues past the threshold. As Jamie looks around, I finally get a good look at him. His eyes are as dark as his unruly hair, which has dried, thanks to the heater in the truck. He brushes a hand over his groomed beard and takes off his black jacket. Damp still clings to his white shirt and holds it against his skin.

Lex clears his throat to stop my staring. I'm not staring because I'm attracted to him—and he *is* attractive—but I want to know more about this strange man from the side of the road. I want to know how his story differs from Lex's . . . and how it's the same.

Lex

I HATE THIS. I fucking hate this. Selena is too good, and it puts her into bad situations. Like the night she met me.

She's too trusting. I've spent a fair bit of my life on the run, hitchhiking from one place to another, but I was *always* on the run from *something* when I held my thumb in the wind. Very few choose to walk along the road and hope for the kindness of strangers. That's not to say everyone who does is up to no good. Not everyone is like me. But the risk of this man being somewhat like me is too high, and it's a chance I didn't want to take. I do things for Selena that I wouldn't do myself, like heading back to New York when I'm wanted there or leaving half the money during a robbery.

"Why do you limp?" I ask as I toss him a dry shirt.

Jamie grabs the shirt and removes the wet one. Selena's eyes land on him again, watching his movements. She's not looking at him like she wants him. She's looking at him as if she's curious about him.

"Military," he says.

I'm not sure I believe him. There's something not wholly trustworthy in his eyes. Or maybe I just don't like Selena's eyes on another man. "You can sleep in that bedroom back there."

He takes a few steps toward the room. I clear my throat, and he stops.

"I have a couple rules."

"Anything, man. What's up?"

"Don't touch anything that doesn't belong to you." I tug Selena into me. "Don't even let her cross your mind. If you even *think* about her, I'll kill you. Do we have an understanding?"

The man nods and turns toward the bedroom. I know he's been at this for a while because he shows little emotion upon hearing my threat. When someone threatens to kill you, your natural instinct is to escape the situation—even Selena responded that way at first—but he's worn down that instinct until it's too dull to react. He just went to the room as if I never said anything at all.

The door closes, and I turn my attention to Selena. "He sure has your attention," I say as I turn toward her and raise her chin.

"Are you jealous, Ben?" she asks, a smirk crossing her sweet face.

I'm not jealous. I'm possessive. Seeing his eyes on her makes me want to go in there and kill him while he sleeps.

"Mind your eyes, little rabbit. I'd hate to see someone killed because you couldn't," I snarl. "Eyes on me, always."

"My eyes are only for you, Lexington," she says with a pout.

I growl and lift her up, wrapping her legs around me. Our clothes are damp, but it cools my skin after it heated up from hearing her say my name. She does *not* want Lexington to come out to play with another man in the house. But she says it again, through a moan as she drops her head back and gives me access to her throat. I bite into her and walk forward until her back hits the wall. I put her down so I can lower her jeans. She slips off her wet shoes and kicks her pants away. I lift her again and kiss her as I work down my jeans and pull my cock out.

"I've wanted you since I saw you bent over in front of that clerk. I love how he wanted you." That's Lexington coming out to play. The same side of me who wanted to see Selena fucked by her piece of shit husband. Lexington loves her, but not like I do. Not in the same way. *I* don't want to see that shit, but I *know* that nagging thought in the back of my mind is from him.

I lay my cock against her pussy. She's still coated in her come, so slick and wet for me. I pull my hips back and push inside her. Her arms wrap around my neck as I thrust deeply, and the warmth of her recently pleasured pussy makes me groan. I lean into her and kiss her as I thrust upward, grinding her back into the wooden wall. She whimpers against my lips. When I go to bite her neck, my eyes catch on a shadow in the darkened doorway.

Jamie.

I can't see his eyes, but I know he's staring. How could he not? Instead of getting angry at him, I take it out on her cunt. I stare at the shadowy figure and rub my hand up the back of her thigh, lifting her leg and gripping her ass. Lexington loves that he's staring at us, and that's the winning feeling as I thrust deeper into her, taking the frustration out on her pussy. The picture frames on the wall above her head rattle with every ounce of the strength I push into her.

The good part of me fights for control. Lexington wants him to watch, wants him to come over here and bury his face in her pussy, but the other side of me recoils at the thought. I told him not to think about her, but how could he think of anything else as he sees the pleasure coursing through her body with every thrust?

"You feel so *fucking* good, rabbit," I growl. She goes to turn her head, but I reach up and keep her eyes on me. Her intense gaze brings me close too quickly. It doesn't help that I've been turned on for the last two hours. "I'm going to come," I tell her. Lexington doesn't give a shit if Selena comes, but the silky cream of her earlier orgasm still coats her pussy.

I pull out of her and put her on her feet. Only once I put her down does she realize Jamie has been watching us. She reaches for her jeans, her mouth gaped in panic, but I grab her arm and keep her from covering herself. Her eyes roll up to mine, and she looks at me like she did back in the kitchen of her old home.

"Lex," she says, slow and cautious, like the prey animal she is.

"Don't just stand there. I know you're watching, and I know what you want," I tell Jamie as I take a step back.

"He doesn't—"

"Now, hitchhiker. Get over here." I raise my voice. From the look in Selena's eyes, I know she fears what's about to happen. Will Lexington ask him to fuck her? Will Lex kill him for looking at what belongs to him?

Maybe both.

Jamie walks over, his eyes darting between us. I grab his shoulder and turn him to face Selena, but she won't look at him.

Good fucking girl.

"I told you not to think about what belongs to me, yet I saw you watching us from the doorway. I know you thought about what it would feel like to sink inside her. Didn't you?"

He tries to turn to face me, his tongue trying to wet his dry lips, but I grip his shirt and force him to keep his eyes on Selena.

"Don't stop watching now, hitchhiker," I snarl. "This is what you wanted to see, so get a good fucking eyeful now."

My skin burns hot with anger. White-hot rage blinds me.

Selena looks at me, and her loose lips tighten. She knows. She tries to speak, but it's too late.

I grip both sides of his head and snap his neck. The thunderous *crack* breaks the silence of the cabin. His death is instantaneous.

She releases a scream I've only heard in her most intense moments of fear. It's not from someone trying to assault her or kill her. It's from a fear of me and what I've done.

Well, Lexington, but for all intents and purposes, it was me.

"Lex!" she yells. "What the fuck?"

I want to go to her, but the anger and fear in her eyes hold me back. This is why Selena isn't safe with me. I'm not always in control. Lexington does all the horrible things to people.

I inhale a sharp breath because I know I'm lying to myself. I've done really horrible shit as Lex, too, but not to her.

Again, I'm not being truthful. I've done some shitty things to her, and I can't blame those things on the man I used to be.

The man that I *am*.

"Bunny," I say, but her panicked breaths wash my voice away. She's crying, afraid to even look at the man she invited into the truck.

I finally step into her and fist her hair to force her to look at him. "This is who I am, Selena. Unpredictable. Dangerous. If I was a fucking dog, they'd put me to sleep. The courts would have loved to give me that sentence, but I lived in a state that didn't believe in capital punishment, even though I deserved that. I still deserve that." My darkened eyes bore into hers. "What I don't deserve is you."

"This is all my fault," she says through sobs. "He died because of me."

I should tell her it's not her fault. But it is. "You're right, Selena. But it's *my* fault for letting you talk me into it. I knew the moment he sat in the truck that he wouldn't leave the cabin alive. I refuse to risk anyone else finding out about where we're staying." My words make her cry harder. "But you can't help being who you are just as much as I can't help being who I am. I'm a person capable of punishing someone for even thinking about what's mine." I shake my head. I pull the truck key from my back pocket and throw it on the table beside her. "I'm going to go take care of this. I expect you to be gone when I get back."

"Wh-what?" she stammers.

She has to leave. Everything that has happened to us since I took her has been because of me. The situations *I've* put her in. I can't keep doing this. She's not safe with me.

No one is.

"I can't create a life that is safe enough for you. It's not possible. We *can't* play house anymore, Selena. You have to leave."

"Lex—"

"Now!" I snap, loud enough to startle her. "If you're not gone by the time I get back, you won't like how I get rid of you."

Like a screw twisting into my heart, it hurts to say these things to her, but if I have to take some pain for her to be safe, so be it.

I've been through worse.

I grab the man's arms and drag him toward the back of the cabin. I look at the kid and wonder where he came from and where he was going. I wish I'd asked more about him. Maybe it would have kept me from doing what I did. But a large part of me knows it wouldn't have mattered. I still would have killed him, even if his body had a backstory attached to it. Now it's just a body that I have to get rid of because I let him inside the truck in the first place.

Because I listened to the pleas of a kind little rabbit.

Chapter Twenty-Two

Selena

Nothing about tonight should have surprised me. Lex is unpredictable. He's always been unpredictable, but he surprised me when he let Jamie watch us. It didn't surprise me when he came to his senses and killed him, though. It was a pendulum, a moment of pleasure before a man was murdered.

The back door slams, and I go to the sink to wash everything off me. My come, Lex's come, the guilt. The way I don't even think about the key on the table until I dry myself off and walk back to my discarded jeans. I put on my pants and stare at the Ford keychain.

I grab the key and button up my jeans, remembering the heat of Lex's touch. I want to leave. Well, a part of me wants to leave. The rest of me is torn. My instinct should be to run, get away from him as fast as I can, but I walk slowly, with hesitation in every step.

My instinct is dull.

Go.
Stay.
Go.

I argue within my mind. I play back everything that happened. The initial carjacking, Lex almost selling me for a piece of plastic, and Lex commanding my husband to fuck me. But I also remember when Lex killed the men for laying hands on me. I remember all the times he pushed me outside my comfort zone and made me feel better than I've ever felt. I've been so alive since the moment he got into my car and told me to drive.

I have a decision to make. And I have to make it now. I grip Lex's pistol and grab the door's handle.

Lex

I PAT the mound of soil with the shovel and breathe in the humid night air. I carry the shovel back toward the cabin and try to reflect on everything. Do I want Selena to leave? Absolutely not. Do I think she should? Yes. I used to think she wasn't safe from everyone else, the other people who are poised to hurt a woman like her, but those aren't the people who've hurt her.

It's been me. Time and time again.

I abducted her. I tried to trade her for a fucking ID. I ignored every no and pushed her until it became a yes. I've made her kill for me and commit robberies. I've almost killed her on so many occasions while trying to protect her from the monsters of the world . . . but I'm the biggest monster of all.

I need her to go. She needs to escape and be a rabbit—blissful, happy, and running free. She doesn't need to be in my cage any longer. She has what she needs to survive now.

To escape the biggest predators.

I lean the shovel against the back porch and head inside the dark cabin. Before I even get to the living room, I see that the tabletop is empty. I release a breath of pained relief. She finally left. She opened her cage and escaped.

The pain in my relief comes from how fucking lost I am without her. She's been all I've known since I escaped prison. I felt things for the first time in a very long time, maybe even my entire life. I had happiness with her.

But I'm not allowed to stay happy. I don't deserve it.

While I escaped the prison for my body, I couldn't escape the prison in my mind. That's a life sentence, and I'll never have freedom from that, even as the most freeing thing lies beneath me. There's no way to turn off who I am. Even for her.

I send a fist through the wall by the back bedroom, and then another. An animalistic scream laced with the frustration I deserve to feel bursts from my throat. I thought I could let her go. When I told her to hate me in the woods, to leave me, there was a part of me that knew she wouldn't, but now she's gone, and I can't handle it.

The anguish turns into anger. Lexington rears his ugly head, trying to blame Selena for what happened. There's no one to blame but him.

Me.

All I can think about is grabbing my gun. I don't know what I'll do once I have it in my hand, but I don't want to do any of this without her. I can't.

The moment I walk through the living room, I hear the sound of the slide racking on my pistol. I turn toward the sound and see Selena behind the silver barrel, staring at me. There's a sharp breath of relief when I see her, but it's short-lived when I take in all the anger on her face. Her eyes are hard and foreign. Her lips are a tight line.

"What is this, rabbit?" I ask as she puts her finger on the trigger. This girl has never handled a gun, and I don't fear she'll willingly shoot me; I fear she'll *accidentally* shoot me while trying to puff her pretty little chest.

"I'm fucking sick of how you treat me," she snarls.

This is *not* how normal couples have this argument. But we aren't normal.

"You aren't going to shoot me, rabbit."

I go for the barrel, but she aims it away from me and pulls the trigger. I don't jump, but she's not used to hearing gunshots and nearly leaps out of her skin at the sound. Splinters of wood break away from the hole in the wall and flutter to the ground.

"You aren't a killer," I say with a laugh.

Her hands shake as she puts the gun back on me. Her finger trembles on the trigger. This girl is going to fucking shoot me in the head on accident. I can't even grab the barrel because she's so damn shaky.

"Why are you upset, Selena? Are you mad because I killed that man?"

"No!" she yells, blowing hair off her forehead in her frustration. "I'm sick of you telling me to leave! I'm tired of worrying about the next thing that happens that makes you push me away!"

I groan. "Really? You're pointing my gun at me because I told you to leave? I was just giving you the freedom you deserve."

I was willing to get on my knees with my gun because I

thought she left. I'd be almost inclined to beg once I got there, if I knew it would make her stay now.

Her finger curls around the trigger, and her eyes narrow. "Do you even care about me?"

Do I? I'd kill *anyone* who hurt her, including myself. I've laid my heart out for her, even if it's not in the way she expects.

I ignore the risk and the anger and deflect the barrel upward as I step into her. I decide to bare my underbelly and try to explain why I'm not always myself.

"I'm sorry for what I did to that man. And to you. There's a battle within me to try to be good for you. It's a whole war inside me. I can't win every battle to be the good guy you sleep with. I'm not even sure which one is the true me, but I'd like to think it's the one who would never lay a hand on your pretty head. But I don't *know*, and that's why I push you away." With a heavy grip on the gun, I wait for her to drop it before I grab it and put it behind my back. I pin her against the wall, lifting her wrists above her head. Her heartbeat crashes against mine. It angered me to no end when she pulled the gun on me. It burned the blood in my veins. But on the same breath, I kind of fucking liked that she did it. She proved her little point.

I lower one of my hands from her wrist and slide it down her body, but she drops her gaze and shakes her head. "No, Lex," she says, and her weakened words prod at Lexington. He loves when she's truly prey. When she's weak. But I keep that side at bay and drop her wrists.

Everything feels so fragile, like a glass balancing on a pin. Forcing her further would knock that glass off its delicate balance.

I lean in and kiss her forehead, tasting the saltiness of

her anxious sweat. "You sleep out here, and I'll go sleep in the bedroom."

We need to make this work. Somehow. Giving her space seems like the only way to do that. Everything is so raw that it will rip us both wide open if we push tonight.

Chapter Twenty-Three

Selena

I wake up in bed without Lex. Last night came to an ugly head for both of us. I had the chance to leave, and I *almost* did. I got in the truck, wrestled with the pistol in my lap, and decided to go back inside. But my anger still ripped through me, coursing through every cell in my body, and that's why I pulled his gun on him. I needed to know why he sometimes seemed like two different people. Why was he always so willing to push me away? Only he could answer that for me.

I climb out of bed and hold my sweat-soaked shirt away from my skin. I hear the water sluggishly running outside. The sound beckons me and when I walk outside, the steamy air assaults me. It grows hot so early in the day here. I follow the sound to the shower stall in the back of the house and find Lex. He's turned away from me as he washes his hair beneath the rusty showerhead. I strip my clothes off and come in behind him. He doesn't turn around at first, his demeanor as cold as the water raining down on me.

"Lex?" I whisper. He puts his hands on the grime-coated wall. I reach around his slick body and rub a hand over his healing stab wound.

"I was a mess when I thought you were gone," he says. His words make me shiver more than the cold water. "I didn't want to live without you, bunny." He finally turns toward me. Water drips from his nose and slides past his full lips. "I'll stop pushing you away if you're sure you can deal with the half of me I *try* to keep from you."

I lean into his broad chest. "Maybe you should stop keeping it from me. I can handle all of you, Lex. I'm not afraid of *you*. The person you become when you try to fight yourself is the one I fear. It's this neck-breaking pendulum of emotions. It's even more erratic when you try to make sense of that part of you. Even if there were a hundred dead bodies around us, I'd love you. Yeah, I was upset when you killed that man, and I felt a lot of guilt, but I wasn't surprised. I expect you to kill a man who thinks about touching me. I knew a clock was ticking above his head. What I don't expect is for you to push me away every time. Like you say to me, stop running from what you are. What you're capable of." I look up at him, blinking away the water as it wets my hair. "I accept all of you, Lexington."

"How, Selena?" He tugs me into him. "How do I deserve you after hurting as many people as I have? After all the times I hurt you? That's what I couldn't figure out yesterday. After everything I've done to you, you still *want* to stay with me. Someone like me doesn't deserve someone so fucking forgiving."

Lex

SELENA CLEANS up and gets out of the shower. She hates the cold water. I stay beneath it for a while longer, reflecting on everything that happened. I stay there until it becomes too much to bear.

I turn off the water and step into the sun. Its powerful rays warm my skin almost immediately. I grab the pair of jeans I set out and pull them on, letting the sun kiss my skin a little longer before heading back inside.

Selena is sitting on the couch in front of a fan, dressed in a pair of black shorts and a cami. Sweat beads on her forehead. I smirk. She doesn't like the cold or the heat. She's a picky little rabbit. She gets off the recliner and steps into me. I wrap my arms around her and forget all that happened between us last night. It's as if we never extinguished someone's life.

Selena is fucking insane for wanting to stay with me, but she's not stupid. Of all the things she is—a little spoiled, stubborn, and bratty—she's not dumb. I need to accept that she's crazy enough to risk her life to be mine. She understands I could hurt her one day. I have to accept that she's unconditionally mine, even when I murder a man for thinking of her.

I lean down and kiss her, tasting the salt of sweat on her lips. I brush her nipples through the thin material of her cami. She shivers at my touch. I grip both sides of her head as I kiss her, and there's not a hint of fear in her, even after she's seen what I've done with nothing more than these two hands.

She moans against my mouth.

"Oh, bunny," I growl, stepping deeper into her and gripping her perfect ass. I hook my fingers into the waistband of her shorts and tug them down. The moment I expose her pale skin, I grow rabid. I'm hungry for her in a way this freedom allows me to be. The freedom we worked so fucking hard for. It's been a long time since I've felt free in any way, even before I got locked up.

I pull off her cami. Her perfect tits relax and spread, and my mouth waters for them.

She pushes me down on the bed. Well, I *let* her push me down. She climbs over my lap, straddling my waist. I grip her hips and move her bare skin along my fly, letting her leave a trail of wetness on my jeans. She moans at the friction.

Her hands reach for my zipper, and I love how her hunger comes through the motions of her fingertips. When I met Selena, she wouldn't have put her hand on me like this or taken charge of her pleasure. I like when my little rabbit becomes a predator when it comes to getting what she wants, especially when she wants my cock.

She pulls my cock from my jeans and when she lowers herself, I feel the end of her. Her absolute limit. She gives me all of her body, just like she always has, as if last night never happened. As if I hadn't killed a man and she hadn't pulled my gun on me.

"Good girl, bunny," I groan as I drop my head back and let myself feel the weight of her on my lap. I listen to her growing moans. We've made love and basked in each other's pleasure so few times.

Her body gleams with sweat as she rides me. She forgets how much she hates the heat when it's me that warms her. Her hands drop to my chest, and she grinds on my lap. I grip her nipples and make her whimper as I squeeze. I pull her chest to mine and kiss her. She spasms around me, squeezing the base of my dick. I pull out so she can tense around my swollen head. I groan and let her pleasure please me. She feels incredible, even once her pussy relaxes and stretches around me.

"God, bunny," I growl. "I can't get enough of your pussy. Can't get enough of you."

"Lexington," she groans.

I look up at her and fight the flicker of frustration as she says my full name again. I don't want him to come and change how I'm fucking her. How she's fucking me. I don't want him to come and fuck her selfishly when I want *her* to be selfish as she chases her orgasm.

There's a darkness that creeps over her expression, completing the transformation into my little wolf with my cock deep inside her.

"Have you ever been spit on?" she asks, a sly grin on her face as she leans forward and rocks on my lap.

Oh, rabbit. "Not the way you're thinking," I say.

"Open your mouth."

I consider shaking my head and telling her no. I'm not into that. I'd spit on her pretty face, in her mouth, on her perfect little cunt, but I'd never considered taking her spit.

But I'll do anything for her, and if she wants to spit in my mouth, I'll let her.

I put my hand behind her neck and drag her toward my mouth. Her lips are so close to mine. I spread my lips and wait for her move. Selena pouts and releases a slow and sensual mouthful of spit that hits my tongue.

Fuck. I didn't think I was into that, but the moment her spit lands in my mouth and she raises herself to ride me, I'm done for.

I pull her down and kiss her again, with our spit still mixing together. I grab her hip with one hand as I coach her movement until she makes me come.

"Dirty fucking rabbit," I growl as I come inside her, filling her as deeply as I can. She doesn't climb off me, not even as my come drips down my shaft and pools on my pelvis. Her hips just rock and coat her pussy in it.

I lift my hip and lay her on her back once more. She kisses me. Someone like her shouldn't let someone like me inside her, let alone allow me to fill her up as much as I have. I've made her take every drop of me since the first time I fucked her.

I pull out of her, and my come drips from her, covering every arch of her perfect pussy. I push her legs apart. "Keep them spread for me," I tell her. Her inner thighs shine with silky cream. "God, I love seeing my come dripping from you. Such a sweet-faced little bunny who has no fucking idea what she's gotten herself into." I run my hand up her thigh, cleaning my come off her skin. "Or maybe you know exactly what you got yourself into and you just don't care."

I push my come back inside her as I lean over and kiss her. I fuck her with my fingers, and the wet sound of our come is like music to my ears. When more drips from her, I drop between her legs and give her a long lick to clean her up. She moans and fists my hair as I curl my tongue and catch every drop.

I sit up and fist her hair, tugging her up until her lips part against the pressure. I spit into her mouth, making her take the last bit of us—our spit *and* our come. She moans and swallows with a bite of her lower lip.

She'll always take everything I give her.

"I love you, Lex," she pants against my mouth as I shove my fingers deep inside her. She releases a moan, and I chase her words with the tips of my fingers. Her chest rises to meet mine.

I've never said I love you to anyone. It feels unnatural.

Too foreign. It's a concept I can't wrap my mind around. I don't understand the word or how it came from her husband's mouth so easily when he clearly didn't love her. How can it matter so much and so little from one person to another? I pull away from her mouth, and the words stick in my throat. I *want* to say it to her—I'm full of that feeling for her—but it's just not as easy for me to say them. I try to show her how I feel, but for a woman like Selena, that will never be enough. She needs to hear it from me, and I'm trying.

I swallow hard. It's as if I am preparing to speak a new language for the first time in front of a room of people. I'll never understand how natural it is for her, how it just rolls off her tongue without a hint of hesitation, especially after everything I've done to her and everything she's witnessed.

I wrap one hand behind her neck and lift her toward my lips. I pull my fingers out of her and put them in her mouth. She takes my come-coated fingers and swallows them whole. God, if that isn't love, I don't know what is.

"I love you, bunny," I let the words roll from my lips and drip into her mouth.

If anyone had told me the scared young thing I carjacked at gunpoint would be the sexy, strong woman beneath me who just spit in my goddamn mouth, I wouldn't have believed them. Not her. Not the sweet little bunny. Now I know what she really is and that she's right where she needs to be.

With me.

Epilogue

Selena

I get into the shower, tugging the old shower curtain across the rusty metal rod. I'll never get used to showering in cold water outside. No matter how cold the water is, my heart is warm because Lex will come in to heat me up.

The curtain moves across the rod, and he's in front of me. Naked already, moonlight illuminates his bare skin. We've been on our own, living away from the confines of our old lives for almost a year now. No matter how long we've been away from it all, my heart still stumbles the moment I see him.

He steps in the small shower, embracing me in his strong arms. "Little rabbit," he growls. Somehow, he never reacts to the cold water, his expression stoic as the frigid droplets rain down on him. My lungs still tighten, shriveling in my chest until my skin becomes numb to the icy finger-tips of the water.

Life with Lex is so different from life with my husband. My ex-husband. Gold woven sheets have become cheap swaths of aged fabric we get from the thrift store. Fancy pantsuits have become cotton shirts and denims on sale. Expensive home-cooked meals have been replaced by what-ever we get on our runs to the general store on the outskirts of the park, where the sweet little owner knows us as Mr. and Mrs. Gurgen Hoffe. Instead of dining out at lavish restaurants, we visit my favorite diner, where half the time I leave pleased with more than just the food in my belly.

Lex's hands leave my body and brush the hair from my face. When his eyes drop to mine, they darken, and my skin pebbles from more than just the cold water. I keep still, like the moment a rabbit freezes and hopes the predator doesn't see them.

He leans into me, drawing his lips close to the shell of my ear. Seduction drips off him like the water droplets from above our heads. "I want to chase you, sweet bunny," he says, low and smooth.

I know he does. I can tell from the way his muscles tense in his upper body. Despite her desperate attempts to freeze, he's spotted the rabbit. He'll chase me until I'm covered in dirt, leaves, and sweat. Or in our come.

"Run," he growls, deep and threatening.

I know who's out to play, and I welcome him.

Lexington.

Lex

THE RABBIT SCURRIES OFF. I nearly lost her by trying to protect her from the darker side of me, so I force myself to stop holding him back. I give in to the unhinged side she loves as much as me, just in a different way.

Selena isn't afraid of Lexington. Even after all she's seen, all she knows, she still likes to call to him while on her knees, as if he won't come out to fuck her throat until she cries.

This side of me courses through my blood like poison. He likes to tell her to run so we can chase her. Whoever catches her decides how she'll be fucked. If Lexington catches her, she's taken rough and hard. If I catch her, we make love until we're covered in mud, leaves, and come.

Losing control has always been easy for me, and she knows that. There's a trail of a bloody past that proves it. For me, keeping control is much harder. And I do try . . . for her. When I fail and the beast inside me roars for her, she doesn't fear me, even when she should. She always takes everything I give her like the good fucking girl she is.

The way she always has.

She used to tell me I never took her from heaven to implant her in hell. She lived among the flames long before she met me. And it's true. But there's something so goddamn innocent about her. It's in the way she laughs as we fall into a habit of game nights instead of robberies or murders. Or when she asks me to explore more of her body in new and exciting ways. She trusts me with every part of her body and, most importantly, her heart.

I'll always say I don't deserve this. Because I don't. Someone like me doesn't deserve someone like her. From hell or heaven, whether fallen or not, she's an angel. She saved me as much as she saved herself.

I know the life I provide her is so different from what

she's used to. It isn't fancy, but it's freedom. I'm free from the confines of prison, and she's free from the hell she once called home.

Studies have shown that sociopaths struggle with attaching to anyone. And I truly never have. I've never *wanted* to. Until her. But they also say that one sociopath could potentially form a bond with a like-minded person. So what does that say about Selena?

She's broken through decades of antisocial and homicidal behavior. She worked her way through the layers of me that psychologists never could. She confronted my past and lived to tell about it. She meets my demons head on with her own, which makes me certain she's so much more than I can ever begin to understand.

Maybe there's not much more to understand.

Maybe she's just as dangerous as me, and my kind of crazy loves hers.

And I wouldn't have it any other way.

I yell into the stiff and silent night. "Ready or not, rabbit, here I come!"

If you want to read another dark hitchhiker romance, check out these two books from Lauren Biel:
Along for the Ride
Books2read.com/MFMHitchhiker
Driving My Obsession
Books2read.com/Drivingmyobsession

Connect with Lauren

Check out LaurenBiel.com to sign up for the newsletter and get VIP (free and first) access to Lauren's spicy novellas and other bonus content!

Join the group on Facebook to connect with other fans and to discuss the books with the author. Visit http://www.face book.com/groups/laurenbieltraumances for more!

Lauren is now on Patreon! Get access to even more content and sneak peeks at upcoming novels. Check it out at www. patreon.com/LaurenBielAuthor to learn more!

Acknowledgments

My husband has been my rock through this entire author journey. Thank you for being there for me through this special book. I love you!

I have to extend a huge thank you again to my unicorn readers and friends! Christina, Kolleen, Sam, Danielle G., Beth, Cheyanna, and Ash, I'm not sure where I'd be without you guys!

Special shout out to my amazing patrons: Amy W., Ariel, Kimberly B., Jay, and Jessica

Lastly, thank you to my editor who helped make this story as perfect as it can be. You're truly amazing!

Also by Lauren Biel

To view Lauren Biel's complete list of books, visit:

www.LaurenBiel.com

or

Campsite.bio/LaurenBielAuthor

About the Author

Lauren Biel is the author of many dark romance books with several more titles in the works. When she's not working, she's writing. When she's not writing, she's spending time with her husband, her friends, or her pets. You might also find her on a horseback trail ride or sitting beside a waterfall in Upstate New York. When reading her work, expect the unexpected.

To be the first to know about her upcoming titles, please visit www.LaurenBiel.com.

Made in the USA
Middletown, DE
26 November 2024